THE WIND IN THE WILLOWS

The Mole had been working hard all the morning.

THE WIND IN THE WILLOWS

KENNETH GRAHAME

abridged and illustrated by

INGA MOORE

CANDLEWICK PRESS
CAMBRIDGE, MASSACHUSETTS

For David, Amelia & Mara

I. M.

Contents

ONE

The River Bank

The Mole had been working hard all the morning, spring-cleaning his little home. First with brooms, then with dusters; then on ladders and steps and chairs, with a brush and a pail of whitewash; till he had dust in his throat and eyes, and splashes of whitewash all over his black fur, and an aching back and weary arms. Spring was moving in the air above and in the earth below, around even his dark and lowly little house, and suddenly he flung down his brush, said "Bother!" and "O blow!" and also "Hang spring-cleaning!" and bolted out of the house without even waiting to put on his coat. Making for the steep tunnel which answered in his case to the gravelled drive owned by animals whose residences are nearer to the sun and air, he scraped and scratched and scrabbled and scrooged, then he scrooged again and scrabbled and scraped, muttering, "Up we go! Up we go!" till at last …

 pop! his snout came out into the sunlight, and he found himself rolling in the warm grass of a great meadow.

"This is fine," he said to himself. "This is better than whitewashing!"

Jumping off all his four legs at once, in the joy of living and spring without its cleaning, he pursued his way across the meadow till he reached the further side.

He rambled busily along the hedgerows, across copses, finding everywhere birds building, flowers budding, leaves thrusting.

As he meandered aimlessly along, suddenly he stood by the edge of a full-fed river. Never in his life had he seen a river before. All was a-shake and a-shiver – gleams and sparkles, chatter and bubble. The Mole was bewitched. By its side he trotted spellbound; and when tired at last, he sat on the bank.

As he sat and looked across to the bank opposite, a dark hole just above the water's edge caught his eye and dreamily he fell to considering what a snug dwelling-place it would make for an animal with few wants and fond of a bijou riverside residence, when something bright and small seemed to twinkle down in the heart of it like a tiny star. But it could hardly be a star. Then, as he looked, it winked at him, and so declared itself to be an eye; and a small face began gradually to grow up round it, like a frame round a picture.

A brown face with whiskers.

A grave round face, with a twinkle in its eye.

Small neat ears and thick silky hair.

It was the Water Rat!

"Hullo, Mole!" said the Water Rat.

"Hullo, Rat!" said the Mole.

"Would you like to come over?" inquired the Rat presently.

"O, it's all very well to *talk*!" said the Mole rather pettishly, he being new to a river and riverside life and its ways.

The Rat said nothing, but stooped and unfastened a rope and hauled on it; then lightly stepped into a little boat. It was painted blue outside and white within and was just the size for two animals; and the Mole's whole heart went out to it at once.

The Rat sculled smartly across and made fast. Then he held up his fore-paw as the Mole stepped gingerly down and, to his surprise, found himself actually seated in the stern of a real boat.

"This has been a wonderful day!" said he, as the Rat shoved off and took the sculls again. "Do you know, I've never been in a boat before in all my life."

"What?" cried the Rat, open-mouthed. "Never been in a — you never — well, I — what have you been doing, then?"

"Is it so nice as all that?" asked the Mole shyly.

"Nice? It's the *only* thing," said the Water Rat solemnly, as he leant forward for his stroke. "Believe me, my friend, there is *nothing* — absolutely nothing — half so much worth doing as simply messing about in boats. Simply messing," he went on dreamily: "messing — about — in — boats; messing — "

"Look ahead, Rat!" cried Mole suddenly.

It was too late. The boat struck the bank full tilt. The Rat lay on his back at the bottom of the boat, his heels in the air.

" — about in boats," he went on, picking himself up with a pleasant laugh. "Look here! If you've really nothing else on this morning, supposing we drop down the river together and have a long day of it?"

The Mole waggled his toes from sheer happiness, spread his chest with a sigh and leaned back blissfully into the soft cushions. "*What* a day I'm having!" he said. "Let us start at once!"

"Hold hard a minute, then!" said the Rat. He looped the painter through a ring in his landing-stage, climbed up into his hole above and reappeared staggering under a fat wicker luncheon-basket.

"Shove that under your feet," he observed to the Mole. Then he untied the painter and took the sculls again.

"What's inside it?" asked the Mole, wriggling with curiosity.

"There's cold chicken inside it," replied the Rat briefly;

"coldtonguecoldhamcoldbeefpickledgherkinssaladfrenchrolls cresssandwichespottedmeatgingerbeerlemonadesodawater—"

"O stop, stop," cried the Mole in ecstasies: "This is too much!"

"Do you really think so?" inquired the Rat seriously. "It's only what I always take and the other animals tell me I'm a mean beast and cut it *very* fine!"

The Mole never heard a word he was saying. Absorbed in the new life, the scents and the sounds and the sunlight, he trailed a paw in the water and dreamed waking dreams. The Water Rat, like the good fellow he was, sculled on.

"I like your clothes awfully, old chap," he remarked after some half hour or so. "I'm going to get a black velvet smoking-suit myself some day."

"I beg your pardon," said the Mole, pulling himself together with an effort. "You must think me very rude; but all this is so new to me. So – this – is – a – River!"

"*The* River," corrected the Rat.

"And you really live by it? What a jolly life!"

"By it and with it and on it and in it," said the Rat. "It's my world, and I don't want any other."

"But isn't it a bit dull at times?" the Mole ventured to ask. "Just you and the river, and no one else to pass a word with?"

"No one else to – well, of course," said the Rat. "You're new to it. The bank is so crowded nowadays that many people are moving away altogether. O no, it isn't what it used to be, at all. Kingfishers, dabchicks, moorhens about all day long always wanting you to *do* something."

"What lies over *there*?" asked the Mole, waving a paw towards a wood that darkly framed the water-meadows on one side.

"That? O, that's just the Wild Wood," said the Rat shortly. "We don't go there very much, we river-bankers."

"Aren't they – aren't they very *nice* people there?" said the Mole a trifle nervously.

"W-e-ll," replied the Rat, "the squirrels are all right. *And* the rabbits – some of 'em, but rabbits are a mixed lot. And then there's Badger. He lives right in the heart of it. Dear old Badger! Nobody interferes with *him*!"

"Why, who *should* interfere with him?" asked the Mole.

"Well, of course – there – are others," explained the Rat. "Weasels – and stoats – foxes – and so on. They're all right in a way, but they break out sometimes, there's no denying it and – you can't really trust them, that's the fact!"

"And beyond the Wild Wood?" asked the Mole.

"The Wide World," said the Rat. "And that doesn't matter."

Leaving the main stream, they passed into what seemed like a land-locked lake. Green turf sloped down to either edge, while ahead of them the silvery shoulder of a weir, arm-in-arm with a mill-wheel, that held up in its turn a grey-gabled mill-house, filled the air with a soothing murmur of sound.

It was so very beautiful that the Mole could only hold up both paws

and gasp, "O my! O my! O my!"

The Rat brought the boat alongside the bank, made her fast, helped the Mole ashore and swung out the luncheon-basket. The Mole begged to be allowed to unpack it all by himself. The Rat was very pleased to indulge him and to sprawl on the grass and rest while his excited friend shook out the tablecloth and spread it, took out the mysterious packets one by one and arranged their contents in due order, still gasping "O my! O my!" When all was ready, the Rat said, "Pitch in, old fellow!" and the Mole was very glad to obey, for he had started his spring-cleaning very early that morning, and had not paused for a bite since.

"What are you looking at?" asked the Rat presently, when the Mole's eyes were able to wander off the tablecloth a little.

"I am looking," said the Mole, "at a streak of bubbles travelling along the surface of the water."

"Bubbles? Oho!" said the Rat.

A broad, glistening muzzle showed itself above the bank, and the Otter hauled himself out and shook the water from his coat.

"Greedy beggars!" he observed. "Why didn't you invite me, Ratty?"

"Such a rumpus everywhere!" he continued. "All the world seems out on the river today. I came up this backwater to get a moment's peace – and stumble on you fellows! At least – I beg your pardon – I don't exactly mean that."

There was a rustle behind them from a hedge, where last year's leaves still clung thick and a stripy head peered forth.

"Come on, old Badger!" shouted the Rat.

The Badger trotted forward a pace or two; then grunted "H'm! Company," turned his back and disappeared.

"That's *just* the sort of fellow he is!" observed the disappointed Rat. "Simply hates Society! We shan't see any more of him today. Well, tell us, *who's* out on the river?"

"Toad's out, for one," replied the Otter. "In his brand-new wager-boat; new togs, new everything!"

The two animals looked at each other and laughed.

"Once, it was nothing but sailing," said the Rat. "Then he tired of that and took to punting. Last year it was house-boating, and we all had to go with him and pretend we liked it. It's all the same, whatever he takes up; he gets tired of it, and starts on something fresh."

"Such a good fellow, too," remarked the Otter. "But no stability – especially in a boat!"

From where they sat they could get a glimpse of the main stream across the island that separated them; and just then a wager-boat flashed into view, the rower – a short stout figure – splashing badly and rolling a good deal, but working his hardest. The Rat stood up and hailed him, but Toad – for it was he – shook his head and settled sternly to his work.

"He'll be out of the boat in a minute," said the Rat, sitting down again.

"Of course he will," chuckled the Otter. "Did I ever tell you that story…"

A Mayfly swerved athwart the current.
A swirl of water and a "cloop!" and
the Mayfly was visible no more.

Neither was the Otter.

Again there was a streak of
bubbles on the surface of the river.

"Well," the Rat said. "I suppose we ought to be moving on.
I wonder which of us had better pack the luncheon-basket?"

"O, let me," said the Mole. So, of course, the Rat let him.

Packing the basket was not quite such pleasant work as
unpacking the basket. It never is. But the Mole was bent on
enjoying everything, and although just when he had got the job
done he saw a plate staring up at him from the grass, and then a
fork which anybody ought to have seen, and last of all the
mustard-pot – still, somehow, the thing got finished at last,
without much loss of temper.

21

The afternoon sun was getting low as the Rat sculled gently homewards, murmuring poetry things, and not paying much attention to Mole. But the Mole was full of lunch, and self-satisfaction, and pride, and already quite at home in a boat (so he thought) and presently he said, "Ratty! Please, *I* want to row!"

The Rat shook his head with a smile. "Not yet," he said. "Wait till you've had a few lessons. It's not so easy as it looks."

The Mole began to feel more and more jealous of Rat, sculling so strongly and easily along. His pride began to whisper he could do it every bit as well, and after a minute or two he suddenly jumped up and seized the sculls. The Rat, who was gazing out over the water, was taken by surprise. He fell backwards off his seat with his legs in the air for the second time, while the triumphant Mole took his place.

"Stop it, you *silly* ass!" cried the Rat from the bottom of the boat. "You'll have us over!"

The Mole flung his sculls back with a flourish and made a great dig at the water. He missed the surface altogether, his legs flew up above his head, and he found himself lying on top of the Rat. He made a grab at the side of the boat and the next moment – Sploosh!

Over went the boat, and he found himself struggling in the water.

O my, how cold the water was, and O, how *very* wet it felt. How it sang in his ears as he went down, down, down! How bright and welcome the sun looked as he rose to the surface. How black was his despair when he found himself sinking again! Then a firm paw gripped him by the back of his neck. It was the Rat, and he was laughing – the Mole could *feel* him laughing, right down his arm and through his paw.

The Rat got hold of a scull and shoved it under the Mole's arm, then he did the same by the other side of him and, swimming behind, propelled him to shore.

The Mole sat on the bank, a squashy lump of misery. When the Rat had rubbed him down a bit, and wrung some of the wet out of him, he said, "Now then, old fellow! Trot up and down the towing-path till you're dry, while I dive for the luncheon-basket."

So the dismal Mole, wet without and ashamed within, trotted about while the Rat plunged into the water again, righted the boat, fetched his floating property and finally dived for the luncheon-basket.

When all was ready the Mole, limp and dejected, took his seat in the stern of the boat. "Ratty!" he said as they set off, in a voice broken with emotion, "I am very sorry. I've been a complete ass, and I know it. To think I might have lost that beautiful luncheon-basket. Will you overlook it this once and let things go on as before?"

"That's all right," said Rat cheerily. "What's a little wet to a Water Rat? I'm more in the water than out of it most days. Don't you think any more about it; look here! I think you had better come and stop with me for a time. I'll teach you to row and swim and you'll soon be as handy on the water as any of us."

The Mole was so touched by his kind manner he could find no voice to answer him; and he had to brush away a tear or two with the back of his paw. But the Rat kindly looked in another direction and soon the Mole's spirits revived and he was even able to give some back-talk to a couple of moorhens who were sniggering to each other about his bedraggled appearance.

When they got home, the Rat made a bright fire in the parlour, and planted the Mole in an arm-chair, in front of it, in dressing gown and slippers, and told him river stories until supper-time. Very thrilling stories they were, too, to an earth-dwelling animal like Mole. Stories about weirs and sudden floods, leaping pike, and herons, adventures down drains and night-fishings with Otter, or excursions far afield with Badger.

Supper was a cheerful meal, but shortly afterwards a terribly sleepy Mole had to be escorted upstairs to the best bedroom, where he laid his head on his pillow in great peace and contentment, knowing that his new-found friend, the River, was lapping the sill of his window.

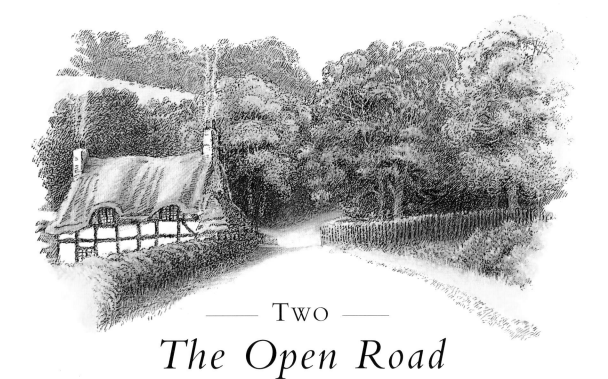

—— TWO ——
The Open Road

"Ratty," said the Mole suddenly, one bright summer morning. "Please, I want to ask you a favour."

The Rat was sitting on the river bank, singing a little song he had just composed about ducks, which he called

DUCK'S DITTY

All along the backwater,
Through the rushes tall,
Ducks are a-dabbling,
Up tails all!

Ducks' tails, drakes' tails,
Yellow feet a-quiver,
Yellow bills all out of sight
Busy in the river!

Everyone for what he likes!
We like to be
Heads down, tails up,
Dabbling free!

"I don't know that I think so *very* much of that little song, Rat," observed the Mole. He was no poet himself and didn't care who knew it. "But what I wanted to ask you was, won't you take me to call on Mr Toad?"

"Why, certainly," said the Rat, jumping to his feet. "Get the boat out at once. It's never the wrong time to call on Toad. He's always glad to see you, always sorry when you go!"

"He must be a very nice animal," observed the Mole, as he got into the boat and took the sculls.

"He is the best of animals," replied Rat. "Perhaps he's not very clever and it may be that he is boastful and conceited. But he has some great qualities, has Toady."

Rounding a bend in the river, they came in sight of Toad Hall, a handsome, dignified old house of mellowed red brick with well-kept lawns reaching down to the water's edge.

They left the boat in the boat-house, and went to look up Toad, whom they happened upon in a wicker garden-chair, a large map spread out on his knees.

"Hooray!" he cried, jumping up. "This is splendid!" He shook their paws. "How *kind* of you! I was just going to send a boat down the river for you, Ratty. I want you badly – both of you."

"It's about your rowing, I suppose," said the Rat. "You're getting on fairly well, and with coaching—"

"O, pooh! boating!" interrupted the Toad. "I've given that up *long* ago. No, I've discovered the real thing! Come with me and you shall see what you shall see!"

He led the way to the stable-yard and there, drawn out of the coach-house, they saw a gipsy caravan, shining with newness, painted a canary-yellow picked out with green, and red wheels.

"There you are!" cried the Toad, straddling and expanding himself. "There's real life for you. The open road, the dusty highway, the heath, the common, the rolling downs! Here today, and off somewhere else tomorrow! The whole world before you! And mind, this is the finest cart of its sort ever built."

The Mole followed him eagerly up the steps and into the caravan. It was very compact and comfortable. Little sleeping-bunks – a table that folded up against the wall – a cooking-stove, lockers, bookshelves and pots, pans, jugs and kettles of every size and variety.

"You see – " said the Toad, pulling open a locker, "biscuits, potted lobster, sardines – everything you can possibly want. Soda-water here – letter-paper there, bacon, jam, cards and dominoes – you'll find," he continued, "that nothing has been forgotten, when we make our start this afternoon."

"I beg your pardon," said the Rat, "but did I hear you say '*we*', and '*start*', and '*this afternoon*'?"

"Dear Ratty," said Toad, "you've *got* to come. I can't manage without you. You don't mean to stick to your river all your life."

"I *am* going to stick to my river," said the Rat. "And what's more, Mole's going to stick to me, aren't you, Mole?"

"I'll always stick to you, Rat," said the Mole loyally. "All the same, it sounds as if it might have been – well, fun!" Poor Mole! He had fallen in love at first sight with the canary-coloured cart and all its little fitments.

The Rat saw what was in his mind and wavered. He was fond of the Mole, and would do almost anything to oblige him. Toad was watching them closely.

"Come along in and have some lunch," he said, "and we'll talk it over. We needn't decide anything in a hurry."

During lunch the Toad simply let himself go, painting the joys of the open life and roadside in such glowing colours that the Mole could hardly sit in his chair for excitement. Somehow, it seemed taken for granted that the trip was a settled thing; and the good-natured Rat could not bear to disappoint his two friends, who were already planning each day for several weeks ahead. The triumphant Toad led his companions to the paddock, and set them to capture the old grey horse, who, to his extreme annoyance, had been told off by Toad for the dustiest job in this expedition. He frankly preferred the paddock, and took a deal of catching. At last he was caught and harnessed and they set off, all talking at once, each animal either trudging by the side of the cart or sitting on the shaft, as the humour took him. It was a golden afternoon. The smell of the dust they kicked up was rich and satisfying; out of orchards on either side the road, birds called and whistled to them cheerily, wayfarers, passing them, gave them "Good day," or stopped to say nice things about their beautiful cart; and rabbits, sitting at their front doors in the hedgerows, held up their fore-paws, and said, "O my!"

Late in the evening, tired and happy and miles from home, they drew up on a remote common, turned the horse loose to graze, and ate their supper sitting on the grass by the side of the cart. Toad talked big about all he was going to do in the days to come, while stars grew fuller all around them …

and a yellow moon, appearing from nowhere in particular,

came to keep them company and listen to their talk.

At last they turned into their little bunks; and Toad, kicking out his legs, sleepily said, "Well, good night, you fellows! This is the life! Talk about your old river!"

"I *don't* talk about my river," replied the Rat. "You *know* I don't, Toad. But I *think* about it," he added. "I *think* about it all the time!" The Mole reached out from under his blanket, felt for the Rat's paw in the darkness, and gave it a squeeze. "Shall we run away tomorrow," he whispered, " – *very* early – and go back to our dear old hole on the river?"

"No, we'll see it out," whispered back the Rat. "I ought to stick by Toad till this trip is ended. It wouldn't be safe for him to be left to himself. It won't take very long. His fads never do."

The end was nearer than even the Rat suspected.

The Toad slept very soundly, and no amount of shaking could rouse him out of bed next morning. So the Mole and Rat turned to, and while the Rat saw to the horse, and lit a fire, and got things ready for breakfast, the Mole trudged off to the nearest village, a long way off, for milk and eggs, which the Toad had, of course, forgotten. The two animals were thoroughly exhausted by the time Toad appeared, fresh and gay, remarking what a pleasant easy life they were leading now, after the cares and worries of housekeeping at home.

They had a pleasant ramble that day over grassy downs, and camped, as before, on a common, only this time the guests took care that Toad should do his share of the work. Next morning their way lay across country by narrow lanes, and it was not till the afternoon that they came out on their first high road; and there disaster sprang out on them.

They were strolling along, the Mole by the horse's head, since the horse had complained that he was being left out of it; the Toad and the Water Rat walking behind the cart talking – at least Toad was talking, and Rat was saying at intervals, "Yes, and what did *you* say to *him*?" – and thinking all the time of something very different, when behind them they heard a warning hum, like the drone of a bee. Glancing back, they saw a small cloud of dust, with a dark centre of energy, advancing on them at incredible speed, while from out of the dust wailed a faint "Poop-poop!"

In an instant the peaceful scene was changed. The "poop-poop" rang with a brazen shout in their ears, and with a blast of wind and a whirl of sound that made them jump for the nearest ditch, the motor-car — its pilot tense and hugging his wheel — was on them. It flung a cloud of dust that blinded them utterly, and then dwindled to a speck in the far distance.

The old grey horse, rearing, plunging, backing steadily, in spite of all the Mole's efforts at his head, drove the cart backwards towards the side of the road. It wavered — then there was a heart-rending crash — and the canary-coloured cart lay on its side in a deep ditch.

"You villains!" shouted the Rat, shaking both fists. "You scoundrels, you — you — road-hogs!"

Toad sat in the middle of the road, his legs stretched out before him, his eyes fixed on the dusty wake of the motor-car. He breathed short, and at intervals murmured "Poop-poop!"

The Mole was trying to quiet the horse. The Rat came to help him. "Hi, Toad!" they cried. "Bear a hand, can't you!"

The Toad never budged. He was in a sort of trance, a happy smile on his face. "The *real* way to travel!" he murmured. "The *only* way to travel! O bliss! O poop-poop! And to think I never *knew*, never even *dreamt*! But *now* – now I know! What dust-clouds shall spring up behind me as I speed on my way! What carts I shall fling into the ditch! Horrid carts – common carts – canary-coloured carts!"

"What are we to do with him?" asked the Mole.

"Nothing," replied the Rat. "You see, I know him of old. He has got a new craze and it always takes him that way, like an animal in a happy dream, quite useless. Never mind him. Let's see about the cart."

A careful inspection showed them that the cart would travel no longer. The axles were in a hopeless state, and one wheel was shattered into pieces.

The Rat took the horse by the head. "Come on!" he said to the Mole. "We shall just have to walk to the nearest town."

"But what about Toad?" asked the Mole.

"O, *bother* Toad," said the Rat.

They had not proceeded very far, however, when there was a pattering of feet behind them, and Toad caught them up.

"Now, look here, Toad!" said the Rat: "as soon as we get to the town, you'll go straight to the police-station, and lodge a complaint against that motor-car."

"Complaint! Me *complain* of that beautiful, heavenly vision! That swan, that sunbeam, that thunderbolt!"

The Rat turned from him in despair. "I give up," he said.

On reaching the town they went straight to the station and deposited Toad in the second-class waiting-room, giving a porter twopence to keep a strict eye on him. They left the horse at an inn stable, and gave what directions they could about the cart. Eventually, a slow train having landed them not far from Toad Hall, they escorted the spellbound Toad to his door. Then they got out their boat and sculled down the river, and at a very late hour sat down to supper in their own cosy parlour.

The following evening the Mole, who had taken things easy all day, was sitting on the bank fishing, when the Rat came strolling along to find him. "Heard the news?" he said. "There's nothing else being talked about, all along the river bank. Toad went up to Town by an early train this morning. And he has ordered a large and very expensive motor-car."

— THREE —
The Wild Wood

The Mole had long wanted to make the acquaintance of the Badger. But whenever he mentioned his wish to the Water Rat he always found himself put off. "Badger'll turn up some day," the Rat would say.

"Couldn't you ask him here – dinner or something?" said the Mole.

"He wouldn't come," replied the Rat simply. "Badger hates Society, and invitations, and dinner, and all that sort of thing."

"Well, supposing we call on *him*?" suggested the Mole.

"O, I'm sure he wouldn't like that at *all*," said the Rat. "He's so very shy. He'll be along some day."

But he never came along, and it was not till summer was over, and cold and frost kept them indoors, that the Mole found his thoughts dwelling again on the grey Badger.

And one cold still afternoon with a hard steely sky overhead, he slipped out of the warm parlour and went by himself to the Wild Wood, where Mr Badger lived.

There was nothing
to alarm him at first entry.
Twigs crackled under his feet, logs
tripped him, funguses on stumps startled him;
but that was all fun, and exciting. It led him on, to
where the light was less, and trees crouched nearer and
nearer, and holes made ugly mouths at him on either side.

Everything was very still now; and the light seemed to be
draining away like flood-water.

Then the faces began.

It was over his shoulder that he first thought he saw a face:
a little evil wedge-shaped face, looking out at him from a hole.
When he turned the thing had vanished.

He quickened his pace, telling himself cheerfully not to
begin imagining things, or there would be simply no end to it.
He passed another hole, and another; then − yes! − no! − yes!
a little narrow face, with hard eyes, had flashed up for an
instant and was gone. He braced himself and strode on. Then
suddenly, every hole, far and near, seemed to possess its face, all
fixing on him glances of malice and hatred: all hard-eyed and
evil and sharp.

If he could only get away from the holes in the banks, he
thought, there would be no more faces. He swung off the path
and plunged into the untrodden places of the wood.

46

Then the whistling began.

Very faint and shrill it was,
when first he heard it;
it made him hurry forward.
Then it sounded far ahead of him,
and made him want to go back.
As he halted it broke out on either side,
and passed throughout the whole length of the wood.
They were up and ready, whoever they were! And he – he was
alone, and unarmed, and far from help;
and the night was closing in.

Then the pattering began.

He thought it was only
falling leaves at first, so
slight was the sound
of it. Then as it grew
it took a rhythm,
and he knew it
for the pat-pat-
pat of little feet.
As he listened anxiously,
leaning this way and that,
it seemed to be closing in on him.
A rabbit came running towards him.
"Get out of this, you fool, get out!" the
Mole heard him mutter as he swung round
a stump and disappeared down a burrow.

The pattering increased till it sounded
like hail on the dry-leaf carpet spread
around him. The whole wood
seemed to be running now,
running hard, hunting,
chasing something
or – somebody?

50

In panic, he began to
run too. He ran
up against
things.

He fell
over things

and
into things.

He darted
under things and

dodged
round things.

At last he took refuge
in the dark hollow of
an old beech tree. He
was too tired to run any
further, and could only
snuggle down into the dry
leaves and hope he was safe
for the time. As he lay panting
and trembling, and listened to the
whistlings and patterings outside, he knew
that dread thing which other little dwellers in
field and hedgerow had encountered here and known
as their darkest moment – the Terror of the Wild Wood!

Meantime the Rat dozed by his fireside. His paper of half-finished verses slipped from his knee, his head fell back and his mouth opened. Then a coal slipped. The fire crackled and he woke with a start. He reached down to the floor for his verses, pored over them for a minute, and then looked round for the Mole to ask him if he knew a good rhyme for something or other.

But the Mole was not there. He listened for a time. The house seemed very quiet.

Then he called "Moly!", got up and went out into the hall. The Mole's cap was missing from its accustomed peg. His goloshes, which always lay by the umbrella-stand, were also gone.

The Rat left the house and examined the muddy ground outside, hoping to find the Mole's tracks. There they were, sure enough. The goloshes were new, just bought for the winter, and the pimples on their soles were fresh and sharp. He could see the imprints of them in the mud, running along straight and purposeful, leading direct to the Wild Wood.

The Rat looked very grave. Then he re-entered the house, strapped a belt round his waist, shoved a brace of pistols into it, took up a stout cudgel that stood in a corner of the hall, and set off for the Wild Wood at a smart pace.

It was already getting towards dusk when he reached the first fringe of trees and plunged without hesitation into the wood, looking anxiously for any sign of his friend. Wicked little faces popped out of holes, but vanished at sight of the Rat, his pistols, and the great ugly cudgel in his grasp; and the whistling and pattering, which he had heard plainly on entry, died away, and all was still. He made his way through the length of the wood, calling cheerfully, "Moly! Where are you? It's me – Rat!"

He had hunted for an hour or more, when he heard a little answering cry. From out of the hole of an old beech tree came a feeble voice, saying, "Ratty! Is that really you?"

The Rat crept into the hollow, and there he found the Mole, exhausted and still trembling. "O Rat!" he cried, "I've been so frightened, you can't think!"

"You shouldn't really have gone and done it, Mole," said the Rat. "We river-bankers hardly ever come here by ourselves. If we have to come, we come in couples; then we're all right. Besides, there are a hundred things to know – passwords, and signs, and plants you carry in your pocket, and verses you repeat, and dodges and tricks; all simple enough when you know them, but they've got to be known if you're small, or you'll find yourself in trouble."

"Surely brave Mr Toad wouldn't mind coming here by himself, would he?" inquired the Mole.

"Old Toad?" said the Rat, laughing heartily. "He wouldn't show his face here for a hatful of guineas."

The Mole was cheered by the sound of the Rat's laughter, as well as by the sight of his stick and his gleaming pistols, and he stopped shivering and began to feel himself again.

"Now then," said the Rat, "we really must make a start for home. It will never do to spend the night here."

"Dear Ratty," said the poor Mole, "I'm simply dead beat. Let me rest a while longer, and get my strength back."

"O, all right," said the Rat. "It's nearly dark now, anyhow; and there ought to be a bit of a moon later."

So the Mole got well into the dry leaves and stretched out, and dropped off into sleep; while the Rat covered himself up for warmth, and lay waiting, with a pistol in his paw.

When at last the Mole woke refreshed and in his usual spirits, the Rat said, "I'll just see if everything's quiet."

He went to the entrance of their retreat and put his head out. Then the Mole heard him saying to himself, "Hullo! hullo! here – *is* – a – go!"

"What's up, Ratty?" asked the Mole.

"*Snow* is up," replied the Rat; "or *down*. It's snowing hard."

The Mole, looking out, saw the wood quite changed. Holes, pitfalls, and other black menaces were vanishing fast, and a gleaming carpet of faery was springing up everywhere.

"Well, it can't be helped," said the Rat. "We must make a start, I suppose. The worst of it is, I don't exactly know where we are. And this snow makes everything look so very different."

It did indeed. The Mole would not have known that it was the same wood. However, they set out bravely, and took the line that seemed most promising.

An hour or two later they pulled up, weary, and hopelessly at sea, and sat down on a fallen tree-trunk. They were aching, and bruised with tumbles; they had fallen into several holes and got wet through; the snow was getting so deep they could hardly drag their little legs through it. There seemed to be no end to this wood, and no beginning, and no difference in it, and, worst of all, no way out.

"We can't sit here," said the Rat. "We shall have to make another push for it. There's a sort of dell down there, where the ground seems all hilly and hummocky. We'll make our way down into that, and try and find some sort of shelter, and we'll have a rest before we try again. Besides, the snow may leave off, or something may turn up."

So they got on their feet, and struggled down into the dell, where they hunted about for a cave or corner that was a protection from the keen wind and the whirling snow, when suddenly the Mole tripped up and fell forward on his face with a squeal.

"O, my leg!" he cried. "O, my poor shin!" and he sat up on the snow and nursed his leg in both his front paws.

"Poor old Mole!" said the Rat kindly. "You don't seem to be having much luck today, do you?"

"I must have tripped over a hidden branch or a stump," said the Mole miserably. "O my! O my!"

"It's a very clean cut," said the Rat, examining it. "That was never done by a branch or a stump. Looks as if it was made by a sharp edge of something metal. Funny!"

"Well, never mind what done it," said the Mole, forgetting his grammar in his pain. "It hurts, whatever done it."

But the Rat, after tying up the leg with his handkerchief, was scraping in the snow.

Suddenly he cried "Hooray! Hooray-oo-ray-oo-ray-oo-ray!" and executed a feeble jig.

"What *have* you found, Ratty?" asked the Mole, hobbling up.

"A door-scraper! Why dance jigs round a door-scraper?"

"But don't you see what it *means*, you – you dull-witted animal?" cried the Rat impatiently.

"Of course I see what it means," replied the Mole. "It means that some *very* careless and forgetful person has left his door-scraper lying about in the middle of the Wild Wood, *just* where it's *sure* to trip *everybody* up!"

"O dear! O dear!" cried the Rat, in despair. "Here, stop arguing and come and scrape!"

After some further efforts, a very shabby door-mat lay exposed to view.

"What did I tell you?" exclaimed the Rat in great triumph.

"Nothing," replied the Mole, with perfect truthfulness. "You seem to have found another piece of domestic litter. Better dance your jig round that, and get it over, then perhaps we can go and not waste any more time over rubbish-heaps. Can we *eat* a door-mat? Or sleep under a door-mat? Or sit on a door-mat and sledge home on it?"

"Do – you – mean – to – say," cried the excited Rat, "that this door-mat doesn't *tell* you anything?"

"Really, Rat," said the Mole pettishly. "Who ever heard of a door-mat *telling* anyone anything? They simply don't do it. They are not that sort at all."

"Now look here, you – you thick-headed beast," replied the Rat, really angry, "this must stop. Not another word. Scrape, scratch and dig, if you want to sleep dry and warm tonight."

The Rat attacked a snow-bank, probing with his cudgel everywhere and digging with fury; and the Mole scraped busily too, more to oblige the Rat than for any other reason, for his opinion was that his friend was getting light-headed.

Some ten minutes' hard work, and the point of Rat's cudgel struck something hollow. He called the Mole to come and help him. Hard at it went the two animals, till at last in the side of what had seemed to be a snow-bank stood a solid-looking little door, painted a dark green. An iron bell-pull hung by the side, and below it, on a small brass plate neatly engraved in square capital letters, they read:

MR BADGER

The Mole fell backwards on the snow from sheer surprise. "Rat!" he cried, "you're a wonder! A real wonder, that's what you are. I see it all now! You argued it out, step by step, in that wise head of yours, from the moment I fell and cut my shin, and you looked at the cut, and your majestic mind said, 'Door-scraper!' And then you found the door-scraper. Did you stop there? No. Some people would have been quite satisfied; but not you. 'Let me find a door-mat,' says you to yourself. And of course you found your door-mat. You're so clever, I believe you could find anything you liked. 'Now to find that door!' says you. Well, I've read about that sort of thing in books, but I've never come across it in real life. You're simply wasted here, among us fellows. If I only had your head, Ratty—"

"But as you haven't," interrupted the Rat rather unkindly, "I suppose you're going to sit on the snow all night and *talk*? Get up and hang on to that bell-pull, and ring as hard as you can, while I hammer!"

While the Rat attacked the door with his stick, the Mole sprang up at the bell-pull, clutched it and swung there, both feet well off the ground, and from quite a long way off they could faintly hear a deep-toned bell respond.

— FOUR —
Mr Badger

They waited patiently for what seemed a very long time, stamping in the snow to keep their feet warm. At last they heard the sound of slow shuffling footsteps approaching the door from the inside. It seemed, as the Mole remarked to the Rat, like someone walking in carpet slippers that were too large for him and down-at-heel; which was intelligent of Mole, because that was exactly what it was.

There was the noise of a bolt shot back, and the door opened a few inches, to show a long snout and a pair of sleepy eyes.

"Now, the *very* next time this happens," said a gruff and suspicious voice, "I shall be exceedingly angry. Who is it *this* time, disturbing people on such a night? Speak up!"

"O, Badger," cried the Rat, "let us in, please. It's me, Rat, and my friend Mole, and we've lost our way in the snow."

"Ratty!" exclaimed the Badger, in quite a different voice. "Come along in, both of you. Why, you must be perished. Well, I never! Lost in the snow! And in the Wild Wood too, at this time of night!"

The two animals tumbled over each other in their eagerness to get inside, and heard the door shut behind them with great joy and relief. The Badger, who wore a long dressing-gown, and whose slippers were indeed very down-at-heel, carried a flat candle-stick and had probably been on his way to bed when their summons sounded. "This is not the sort of night for small animals to be out," he said. "I'm afraid you've been up to some of your pranks again, Ratty."

He shuffled on in front of them, carrying the light, and they followed him down a long, and to tell the truth, decidedly shabby passage, into a sort of a hall, out of which they could see other passages branching mysteriously. There were doors as well – stout oaken doors. One of these the Badger flung open, and they found themselves in all the glow and warmth of a large fire-lit kitchen.

The kindly Badger thrust them down on a settle to toast themselves at the fire, and bade them remove their wet coats and boots. Then he fetched them dressing-gowns and slippers, and bathed the Mole's shin with warm water and mended the cut with sticking-plaster till the whole thing was as good as new, if not better. Warm and dry at last, with weary legs propped up in front of them, it seemed to the storm-driven animals that the cold and trackless Wild Wood just left outside was miles and miles away, and all that they had suffered in it a half-forgotten dream.

When at last they were thoroughly toasted, the Badger summoned them to the table. They had felt pretty hungry before, but when they saw the supper spread for them, it seemed only a question of what they should attack first where all was so attractive, and whether the other things would wait till they had time to give them attention. Conversation was impossible for a long time; and when it was resumed, it was that regrettable sort that results from talking with your mouth full. The Badger did not mind that sort of thing at all, nor did he take any notice of elbows on the table, or everybody speaking at once. As the animals told their story, he did not seem surprised or shocked at anything. He never said, "I told you so," or, "Just what I always said," or remarked that they ought to have done so-and-so, or ought not to have done something else. The Mole began to feel very friendly towards him.

Supper finished, they gathered round the glowing embers of the great fire, and thought how jolly it was to be sitting up *so* late, and *so* full; and after they had chatted for a time, the Badger said, "Well, it's time we were all in bed." He conducted the two animals to a long room that seemed half bedchamber and half loft. The Badger's winter stores took up half the room, but the two little beds on the remainder of the floor looked soft and inviting, and the linen on them, though coarse, was clean and smelt beautifully of lavender; and the Mole and the Water Rat, shaking off their garments in some thirty seconds, tumbled in between the sheets in great joy and contentment.

The two tired animals
came down to breakfast
very late next morning,
and found a bright fire
burning in the kitchen,
and two young
hedgehogs sitting
on a bench at
the table, eating
oatmeal porridge
out of wooden
bowls.

The hedgehogs dropped their spoons and rose to their feet respectfully as the two entered.

"Sit down, sit down," said the Rat pleasantly, "and go on with your porridge. Where have you youngsters come from? Lost your way in the snow, I suppose?"

"Yes, please, sir," said the elder of the two hedgehogs. "Me and Billy was trying to find our way to school and we lost ourselves, sir, and Billy got frightened and took and cried, being young. And we happened up against Mr Badger's back door, and knocked, sir, for Mr Badger he's a kind-hearted gentleman, as everyone knows—"

"I understand," said the Rat, cutting himself some rashers of bacon, while the Mole dropped some eggs into a saucepan. "And what's the weather like outside? You needn't 'sir' me quite so much," he added.

"O, terrible bad, sir, terrible deep the snow is," said the hedgehog. "No getting out for you gentlemen today."

"Where's Mr Badger?" inquired the Mole.

"The master's gone into his study, sir," replied the hedgehog, "and said as how he was going to be particular busy this morning, and on no account was he to be disturbed."

The animals well knew that Badger, having eaten a hearty breakfast, had retired to his study and settled himself in an arm-chair with his legs on another and a red cotton handkerchief over his face, and was being "busy" in the usual way at this time of the year.

The front-door bell clanged loudly, and the Rat, who was very greasy with buttered toast, sent Billy, the smaller hedge-hog, to see who it might be. There was a sound of much stamping in the hall, and presently Billy returned in front of the Otter, who threw himself on the Rat with a shout.

"Get off!" spluttered the Rat, with his mouth full.

"Thought I should find you here," said the Otter cheerfully. "They were all in a state along River Bank this morning. Rat never been home all night – nor Mole either – something dreadful must have happened, they said; and the snow had covered your tracks. But I knew when people were in any fix they mostly went to Badger, so I came straight here, through the Wild Wood. About halfway across I came on a rabbit sitting on a stump, cleaning his silly face. I managed to extract from him that Mole had been seen in the Wild Wood last night. It was the talk of the burrows, he said, how Mole, Mr Rat's particular friend, was in a bad fix; how he had lost his way, and 'They' were up and out hunting, and were chivvying him round and round. 'Why didn't you *do* something?' I asked. 'What, us?' he said: '*do* something? us rabbits?' So I cuffed him. There was nothing else to be done. At any rate, I had learnt something; and if I had had the luck to meet 'Them' I'd have learnt something more – or *they* would."

"Weren't you – er – nervous?" asked the Mole.

"Nervous?" The Otter laughed. "I'd give 'em nerves if any of them tried anything on with me. Here, Mole, fry me some slices of ham. I'm hungry, and I've any amount to say to Ratty here. Haven't seen him for an age."

So the good-natured Mole, having cut some slices of ham, set the hedgehogs to fry it, and returned to his own breakfast, while the Otter and the Rat talked river-shop.

A plate of fried ham had just been cleared and sent back for more, when the Badger entered, yawning and rubbing his eyes, and greeted them. "It must be getting on for luncheon time," he remarked to the Otter. "Better stop and have it with us. You must be hungry, this cold morning."

"Rather!" replied the Otter, winking at the Mole.

The hedgehogs, who were just beginning to feel hungry again after working so hard at their frying, looked timidly up at Mr Badger, but were too shy to say anything.

"You be off to your mother," said the Badger kindly. "I'll send someone with you to show you the way."

He gave them sixpence apiece and they went off.

Presently they all sat down to luncheon together. The Mole found himself next to Mr Badger, and, as the other two were still deep in river-gossip, he took the opportunity to tell Badger how home-like it all felt to him. "Once underground," he said, "you know exactly where you are. Nothing can happen to you, and nothing can get at you. Things go on all the same overhead, and you don't bother about 'em. When you want to, up you go, and there the things are, waiting for you."

The Badger beamed on him. "That's exactly what I say," he replied. "There's no security, or peace, except underground. Look at Rat, now. A couple of feet of flood-water, and he's got  to move into hired lodgings. Take Toad. I say nothing against Toad Hall; quite the best house in these parts, *as* a house. But supposing a fire breaks out – where's Toad? Supposing tiles are blown off, or windows get broken – where's Toad? No, up and out of doors is good enough to roam about and get one's living in; but underground – that's my idea of *home*!"

The Mole assented heartily; and the Badger got very friendly with him. "When lunch is over," he said, "I'll take you round this little place of mine."

Accordingly, when the other two had settled themselves into the chimney-corner and had started a heated argument on the subject of *eels*, the Badger lighted a lantern and bade the Mole follow him. Crossing the hall, they passed down one of the tunnels, and the wavering light gave glimpses on either side of rooms, some mere cupboards, others nearly as broad and imposing as Toad's dining-hall. A passage at right angles led into another corridor, and here the same thing was repeated. The Mole was staggered at the size of it all; at the length of the dim passages, the vaultings, the pillars, the arches.

"How on earth, Badger," said the Mole at last,

"did you do all this? It's astonishing!"

"It *would* be astonishing," said the Badger, "if I *had* done it. But as a matter of fact I did none of it – only cleaned out the passages, as I had need of them. You see, long ago, on the spot where the Wild Wood waves now, before ever it had planted itself and grown, there was a city – a city of people, you know. Here, where we are standing, they walked, and talked, and carried on their business. They were a powerful people, and rich, and great builders."

"But what has become of them all?" asked the Mole.

"Who can tell?" said the Badger. "People come – they stay for a while – and they go. But we remain. There were badgers here long before that same city ever came to be. And now there are badgers here again."

When they got back to the kitchen again, they found the Rat very restless. The underground atmosphere was getting on his nerves, and he seemed to be afraid that the river would run away if he wasn't there to look after it. He had his overcoat on, and his pistols thrust into his belt again. "Come along, Mole," he said. "We must get off while it's light. Don't want to spend another night in the Wild Wood."

"It'll be all right," said the Otter. "I'm coming with you. I know every path blindfold; and if there's a head to be punched, you can rely upon me to punch it."

"You needn't fret, Ratty," added the Badger. "My passages run further than you think, and I've bolt-holes to the edge of the wood in several directions, though I don't care for everybody to know about them. When you really have to go, you shall leave by one of my short cuts."

The Rat was still anxious to be off, so the Badger, taking up his lantern again, led the way along a damp and airless tunnel that wound and dipped for what seemed to be miles. At last daylight began to show itself through tangled growth overhanging the mouth of the passage; and the Badger, bidding them a hasty good-bye, pushed them through, made everything look as natural as possible again, with brushwood, and dead leaves, and retreated.

They found themselves standing on the very edge of the Wild Wood. Rocks and brambles and tree-roots behind them; in front, a great space of fields, hemmed by lines of hedges black on the snow, and, far ahead, a glint of the familiar old river, while the wintry sun hung red and low on the horizon. They trailed out on a bee-line for a distant stile. Pausing there and looking back, they saw the whole of the Wild Wood, menacing, compact, grimly set in vast white surroundings; they turned and made for home, for firelight and the familiar things it played on, for the voice of the river they knew and trusted, that never made them afraid.

As he hurried along, the Mole saw clearly he was an animal of field and hedgerow, the ploughed furrow, the frequented pasture, the lane of evening lingerings, the cultivated garden-plot. For others the conflict that went with Nature in the rough; he must be wise, must keep to the places in which his lines were laid and which held adventure enough, in their way, to last for a lifetime.

— FIVE —

Dulce Domum

The sheep ran huddling together against the hurdles, blowing out thin nostrils and stamping with delicate forefeet, their heads thrown back and a light steam rising from the crowded sheep-pen into the frosty air, as the two animals hastened by in high spirits. They were returning across country after a day's outing with Otter, and the shades of the short winter day were closing in. They had heard the sheep and had made for them; and now, leading from the sheep-pen, they found a beaten track.

"It looks as if we're coming to a village," said the Mole, slackening his pace.

"O, at this season of the year," said the Rat, "they're safe indoors by this time, men, women, children and all. We shall slip through without any bother."

The rapid nightfall of mid-December had quite beset the little village as they approached it on soft feet over a first thin fall of powdery snow. Little was visible but squares of a dusky orange-red on either side of the street, where the firelight or lamplight of each cottage overflowed through the casements into the dark world without. Most of the low latticed windows were innocent of blinds, and moving from one to another, the lookers-in, so far from home themselves, watched a cat being stroked, a sleepy child picked up and huddled off to bed, or a tired man stretch and knock out his pipe on the end of a smouldering log.

But it was from one little window, with its blind drawn down, that the sense of home most pulsated. Against the blind hung a bird-cage, clearly silhouetted. On the perch, the fluffy occupant, head tucked well into feathers, seemed so near to them as to be easily stroked, had they tried. As they looked, the sleepy little fellow stirred, shook himself, and raised his head. They could see the gape of his tiny beak as he yawned in a bored sort of way, looked around, and settled again. Then a gust of bitter wind took them in the back of the neck, a small sting of frozen sleet woke them as from a dream, and they knew their toes to be cold and their legs tired, and their own home distant a weary way.

Once beyond the village, they could smell the friendly fields again; and they braced themselves for the last long stretch, the home stretch, the stretch that we know is bound to end in the rattle of the door-latch, sudden firelight, and the sight of familiar things greeting us. They plodded along steadily and silently, each of them thinking his own thoughts. The Mole's ran a good deal on supper, as it was pitch dark, and it was all strange country to him as far as he knew. The Rat was walking a little way ahead, his eyes fixed on the road in front of him; so he did not notice Mole when the summons reached him, and took him like an electric shock.

We have only the word "smell" for the whole range of delicate thrills which murmur in the nose of the animal night and day. It was one of these mysterious fairy calls that suddenly reached Mole in the darkness, making him tingle through and through. He stopped dead in his tracks, his nose searching hither and thither.

Home! That was what they meant, those soft touches wafted through the air, those invisible little hands pulling and tugging, all one way! Why, it must be quite close by him at that moment, his old home he had forsaken when he first found the river! Since that bright morning he had hardly given it a thought. Shabby and poorly furnished, and yet his, the home he had made for himself, the home he had been so happy to get back to after his day's work. And the home was missing him, and wanted him back, and was telling him so, through his nose, sorrowfully, but with no bitterness or anger; that it was there, and wanted him.

"Ratty!" he called. "Come back! I want you, quick!"

84

"O, *come* along, Mole!" replied the Rat, plodding along.

"Stop, Ratty!" pleaded the Mole. "You don't understand! It's my home, my old home! I've just come across the smell of it, and it's really quite close. Come back, Ratty! Please!"

The Rat was by this time very far ahead, too far to hear what the Mole was calling.

"We mustn't stop now!" he called back. "It's late, and the snow's coming on again, and I'm not sure of the way! And I want your nose, Mole, so come on, there's a good fellow!" And the Rat pressed on without waiting for an answer.

Poor Mole stood alone in the road, his heart torn asunder, a big sob gathering, somewhere low down inside him. Never for a moment did he dream of abandoning his friend. His old home pleaded, whispered. With a wrench he followed in the track of the Rat, while faint, thin little smells, still dogging his nose, reproached him for his forgetfulness.

He caught up the Rat, who began chattering about what they would do when they got back, and how jolly a fire in the parlour would be, and what a supper he meant to eat; never noticing his companion's silence. At last, when they were passing some tree-stumps at the edge of a copse, he stopped and said kindly, "Look here, Mole, old chap, you seem dead tired. No talk left in you, and your feet dragging like lead. We'll sit down here for a minute and rest. The snow has held off, and the best part of our journey is over."

The Mole tried to control himself, for he felt it coming, the sob he had fought so long. Up and up, it forced its way to the air, and then another, and another, and others thick and fast; till poor Mole at last gave up the struggle, and cried helplessly, now that he knew it was all over and he had lost what he could hardly be said to have found.

The Rat did not dare to speak for a while. At last he said, "What is it, old fellow? Whatever can be the matter?"

Mole found it difficult to get any words out. "I know it's a — shabby, little place," he sobbed at last: "not like — your cosy quarters — or Toad's beautiful hall — or Badger's great house — but it was my own little home — and I was fond of it — and then I smelt it suddenly — on the road, when I called and you wouldn't listen, Rat. — We might have just gone and had one look at it — but you wouldn't turn back, you wouldn't!"

The Rat stared in front of him, saying nothing. After a time he muttered, "What a *pig* I have been! A *pig* — that's me!"

Then he rose, and, remarking, "Well, we'd better be getting on!" set off up the road again, the way they had come.

"Wherever are you (hic) going to, Ratty?" cried the Mole.

"We're going to find that home of yours, old fellow," replied the Rat pleasantly.

"Come back, Ratty, do!" cried the Mole, hurrying after him. "The snow's coming! Think of River Bank, and your supper!"

"Hang River Bank!" said the Rat heartily.

When it seemed they must be nearing that part of the road where the Mole had been "held up", Rat said, "Now! Use your nose!"

Mole stood a moment rigid. His uplifted nose, quivering slightly, felt the air.

Then a short, quick run forward — a fault — a check — a try back; and then a slow, steady, confident advance.

The Rat kept close to his heels as the Mole, with something of the air of a sleep-walker, crossed a dry ditch, scrambled through a hedge, and nosed his way over a field open and trackless and bare in the faint starlight.

Suddenly he dived; the Rat promptly followed him down the tunnel to which his unerring nose had faithfully led him.

It was close and airless, and the earthy smell was strong. The Mole struck a match, and by its light the Rat saw that they were standing in an open space, neatly swept and sanded underfoot, and directly facing them was Mole's little front door, with "Mole End" painted, in Gothic lettering, over the bell-pull at the side.

Mole reached down a lantern from a nail on the wall and lit it, and the Rat, looking round him, saw that they were in a sort of fore-court. A garden-seat stood on one side of the door, and on the other, a roller; for the Mole, who was a tidy animal, could not stand having his ground kicked up into earth-heaps. On the walls hung wire baskets with ferns in them, brackets carrying plaster statuary – Garibaldi, and the infant Samuel, and Queen Victoria, and other heroes of modern Italy. Down one side of the fore-court ran a skittle-alley, with benches along it and little wooden tables. In the middle was a small pond containing goldfish and surrounded by a cockle-shell border. Out of the centre of the pond rose a fanciful erection clothed in more cockle-shells and topped by a large silvered glass ball that reflected everything all wrong and had a very pleasing effect.

Mole's face beamed at the sight of all these objects so dear to him, and he hurried Rat through the door, lit a lamp in the hall, and took one glance round his old home. He saw the dust lying thick on everything, saw the cheerless, deserted look of the long-neglected house, and its worn and shabby contents – and collapsed again on a hall-chair, his nose in his paws.

"O, Ratty!" he cried dismally, "why ever did I do it? Why did I bring you to this poor, cold place, when you might have been at River Bank, with all your nice things about you!"

The Rat was running here and there, opening doors, and cupboards; lighting lamps and candles and sticking them up everywhere. "What a capital little house this is!" he called out cheerily. "We'll make a jolly night of it. The first thing we want is a good fire; I'll see to that. You get a duster, Mole, and try and smarten things up a bit."

Encouraged by his companion, the Mole roused himself and dusted with energy, while the Rat soon had a cheerful blaze roaring up the chimney. But Mole had another fit of the blues, dropping on a couch and burying his face in his duster.

"Rat," he moaned, "you poor, hungry, animal. I've nothing to give you – nothing – not a crumb!"

"What a fellow you are for giving in!" said the Rat. "Why, only just now I saw a sardine-opener on the kitchen dresser, quite distinctly; and everybody knows that means there are sardines about somewhere. Come with me and forage."

They went hunting through every cupboard and drawer. The result was not so depressing after all, though of course it might have been better; a tin of sardines – a box of captain's biscuits, nearly full – and a German sausage in silver paper.

The Rat busied himself fetching plates, knives and forks, and mustard which he mixed in an egg-cup, and had just got seriously to work with the sardine-opener when sounds were heard from the fore-court without – like the scuffling of small feet in the gravel and a murmur of tiny voices – "All in a line – hold the lantern up a bit, Tommy – no coughing after I say one, two, three. – Come on, we're all a-waiting—"

"What's up?" inquired the Rat.

"I think it must be the field-mice," replied the Mole, with a touch of pride in his manner. "They go round carol-singing regularly at this time of year. They're quite an institution in these parts. And they never pass me over – they come to Mole End last of all; and I used to give them hot drinks, and supper too sometimes, when I could afford it. It will be like old times to hear them again."

"Let's have a look at them!" cried the Rat, jumping up and running to the door.

In the fore-court, lit by the dim rays of a horn lantern, some eight or ten little field-mice stood in a semicircle, red worsted comforters round their throats, their fore-paws thrust deep into their pockets, their feet jigging for warmth. With bright beady eyes they glanced shyly at each other, sniggering a little, sniffing and applying coat-sleeves a good deal.

As the door opened, their shrill little voices uprose on the air.

Carol

Villagers all, this frosty tide,
Let your doors swing open wide,
Though wind may follow,
    and snow beside,
Yet draw us in by your fire to bide;
Joy shall be yours in the morning!

Here we stand in the cold and sleet,
Blowing fingers and stamping feet,
Come from far away you to greet –
You by the fire and we in the street –
Bidding you joy in the morning!

"Well sung!" cried the Rat. "And now come along in, all of you, and have something hot!"

"Yes, come along, field-mice," cried the Mole eagerly. "You just wait a minute, while we – O, Ratty!" he cried in despair. "Whatever are we doing? We've nothing to give them!"

"You leave all that to me," said the Rat. "Here, you with the lantern! Are there any shops open at this hour of the night?"

"Certainly, sir," replied the field-mouse respectfully. "At this time of year our shops keep open to all sorts of hours."

"Then you go off at once," said the Rat, "and get me—"

Here the Mole only heard "Fresh, mind! – no, a pound will do – only the best – if you can't get it there, try somewhere else – of course, home-made, no tinned stuff – well, do the best you can!" There was a chink of coin passing from paw to paw, the field-mouse was provided with a basket for his purchases, and off he hurried, he and his lantern.

The rest of the field-mice perched in a row on the settle, their small legs swinging.

"They act plays too," the Mole explained to the Rat. "Make them up all by themselves. They gave us a capital one last year, about a field-mouse who was captured at sea and made to row in a galley; and when he escaped and got home, his lady-love had gone into a convent. Here, you were in it, I remember. Get up and recite a bit."

The field-mouse addressed got up on his legs, giggled shyly, looked round the room, and remained absolutely tongue-tied. His comrades cheered him on, Mole coaxed him, but nothing could overcome his stage-fright. Then the door opened, and the field-mouse with the lantern reappeared, staggering under the weight of his basket.

In a few minutes supper was ready, and Mole, as he took the head of the table, saw his little friends' faces brighten and beam as they fell to and thought what a happy home-coming this had turned out, after all. As they ate, they talked of old times,

and the field-mice gave him the local gossip up to date, and answered as well as they could the hundred questions he had to ask them. The Rat said little or nothing, only taking care that each guest had what he wanted, and plenty of it, and that Mole had no trouble or anxiety about anything.

They clattered off at last, with their jacket pockets stuffed with remembrances for the small brothers and sisters at home. When the door had closed on the last of them and the chink of the lanterns had died away, Mole and Rat kicked the fire up, drew their chairs in, and discussed the events of the long day. At last the Rat, with a tremendous yawn, said, "Mole, old chap, I'm ready to drop. Sleepy is simply not the word. That your own bunk over on that side? Very well, then, I'll take this. What a ripping little house this is! Everything so handy!"

He clambered into his bunk and rolled himself well up in the blankets, and slumber gathered him forthwith.

The weary Mole also soon had his head on his pillow. But ere he closed his eyes he let them wander round his old room, mellow in the glow of the firelight that played on familiar and friendly things. He saw clearly how plain and simple — how narrow, even — it all was; but clearly, too, how much it all meant to him. He did not at all want to abandon the new life, to turn his back on sun and air; the upper world was all too strong, it called to him still, even down there, and he knew he must return. But it was good to think he had this to come back to, this place which was all his own, these things which were so glad to see him again and could always be counted upon for the same simple welcome.

SIX

Mr Toad

It was a bright morning in the early part of summer; the river had resumed its wonted banks, and a hot sun seemed to be pulling everything green and bushy up out of the earth, as if by strings. The Mole and the Water Rat had been up since dawn, busy on matters connected with boats and the boating season; painting and varnishing, mending paddles, repairing cushions, hunting for missing boat-hooks, and so on; and were finishing breakfast in their little parlour and discussing their plans for the day, when a heavy knock sounded at the door.

"Bother!" said the Rat, all over egg. "See who it is, Mole, like a good chap, since you've finished."

The Mole went to attend the summons, and the Rat heard him utter a cry of surprise. Then he flung the parlour door open, and announced with much importance, "Mr Badger!"

This was a wonderful thing, indeed, that the Badger should call on them, or on anybody. He generally had to be caught, if you wanted him, as he slipped quietly along a hedgerow of an early morning or a late evening, or else hunted up in his own house in the middle of the wood.

The Badger strode into the room, and stood looking at the two animals with an expression full of seriousness.

"The hour has come!" he said.

"What hour?" asked the Rat uneasily, glancing at the clock.

"*Whose* hour, you should say," replied the Badger. "Why, Toad's hour! The hour to take Toad in hand!"

"Hooray!" cried the Mole delightedly. "*We'll* teach him to be a sensible Toad!"

"This very morning," continued the Badger, "another new and exceptionally powerful motor-car will arrive at Toad Hall on approval or return."

"We ought to do something," said the Rat gravely. "He had another smash-up only last week, and a bad one. That coach-house of his is piled to the roof with fragments of motor-cars, none of them bigger than your hat!"

"He's been in hospital three times," put in the Mole; "and as for the fines he's had to pay, it's simply awful to think of."

"Yes," continued the Rat, "Toad's rich, we all know; but he's not a millionaire. And he's a hopelessly bad driver, and quite regardless of law and order. Killed or ruined – it's got to be one of the two, sooner or later."

"We must be up and doing," said the Badger, "ere it is too late. You two will accompany me instantly to Toad Hall."

"Right you are!" cried the Rat, starting up. "We'll rescue the poor animal!"

"We'll take him seriously in hand," went on the Badger. "We'll stand no nonsense whatever. We'll bring him back to reason, by force if need be. We'll *make* him be a sensible Toad."

They set off up the road on their mission, and reached Toad Hall to find, as the Badger had anticipated, a shiny new motor-car, of great size, painted a bright red, standing in front of the house. As they neared the door it was flung open, and Mr Toad, arrayed in goggles, cap, gaiters, and enormous overcoat, came swaggering down the steps.

"Hullo! you fellows!" he cried. "You're just in time to come for a jolly – a jolly – for a – er jolly—"

The Badger strode up the steps. "Take him inside," he said to his companions. Then he turned to the chauffeur in charge of the new motor-car.

"I'm afraid you won't be wanted today," he said. "Mr Toad has changed his mind. He will not require the car."

"Now, then!" he said to the Toad, when the four of them stood in the hall, "first, take those ridiculous things off!"

"Shan't!" replied Toad, with spirit. "What is the meaning of this? I demand an explanation."

They had to lay Toad out on the floor, kicking and calling all sorts of names, before they could get his motor-clothes off him bit by bit, and they stood him up on his legs again. Now he was merely Toad, and no longer the Terror of the Highway, he giggled feebly.

"You knew it must come to this sooner or later, Toad," the Badger explained severely. "You've disregarded all the warnings we've given you, you're getting us animals a bad name in the district by your furious driving and your smashes and your rows with the police. But we never allow our friends to make fools of themselves beyond a certain limit; and that limit you've reached. You've often asked us to come and stay with you, Toad; well, now we're going to. When you are sorry for what you've done, and see the folly of it, and you promise never to touch a motor-car again, we may quit, but not before. Take him upstairs, you two, and lock him in his bedroom."

"It's for your own good, Toady," said the Rat kindly, as Toad, kicking and struggling, was hauled upstairs by his two friends. "Think what fun we shall all have together, just as we used to, when you've quite got over this – this painful attack of yours! No more of those incidents with the police," he said, as they thrust him into his bedroom.

"No more weeks in hospital, being ordered about by nurses," added the Mole, turning the key on him.

They descended the stair, Toad shouting abuse at them through the keyhole.

"It's going to be a tedious business," said the Badger, sighing. "I've never seen Toad so determined. However, we will see it out. He must never be left an instant unguarded. We shall take it in turns to be with him, till the poison is out of his system."

They arranged watches accordingly. Each animal took turns to sleep in Toad's room at night, and they divided the day between them. At first Toad was very trying to his guardians. He would arrange bedroom chairs in rude resemblance of a motor-car and crouch on them, bent forward, staring fixedly ahead, making uncouth, ghastly noises, till the climax was reached, when, turning a complete somersault, he would lie prostrate amidst the ruins of the chairs, completely satisfied for the moment. As time passed, however, these seizures grew less frequent, and his friends strove to divert his mind into fresh channels. But his interest in other matters did not seem to revive, and he grew apparently languid and depressed.

One fine morning the Rat, whose turn it was to go on duty, went upstairs to relieve Badger, whom he found fidgeting to be off and stretch his legs. "Toad's still in bed," he told the Rat, outside the door. "Can't get much out of him, except, 'O, leave him alone.' Now, you look out, Rat! When Toad's quiet, he's at his artfullest."

"How are you today, old chap?" inquired the Rat cheerfully, as he approached Toad's bedside.

A feeble voice replied, "Thank you, Ratty! So good of you to inquire! How are you yourself, and the excellent Mole?"

"O, *we're* all right," replied the Rat. "Mole is going out for a run with Badger. So you and I will spend a pleasant morning together. Now jump up, there's a good fellow!"

"Dear Rat," murmured Toad, "I am far from 'jumping up'. I beg you – step round to the village and fetch the doctor."

"What do you want a doctor for?" inquired the Rat, coming closer and examining him. He certainly lay very still and flat, and his voice was weaker and his manner changed.

"Surely you have noticed—" murmured Toad. "Tomorrow, indeed, you may be saying, 'O, if only I had noticed sooner! If only I had done something!' But never mind – forget I asked."

"Look here, old man," said the Rat, beginning to get rather alarmed, "of course I'll fetch a doctor, if you really want him."

"And – would you mind," said Toad, with a sad smile, "at the same time asking the lawyer to step up? There are moments – a moment – when one must face disagreeable tasks."

"A lawyer! He must be bad!" the Rat said to himself, as he hurried from the room, not forgetting to lock the door behind him. "I've known Toad fancy himself frightfully bad before; but I've never heard him ask for a lawyer! If there's nothing the matter, the doctor will tell him he's an old ass, and cheer him up. I'd better go; it won't take long." So he ran off to the village on his errand of mercy.

Mr Toad

The Toad, who had hopped lightly out of bed as soon as he heard the key turned in the lock, watched him from the window till he disappeared down the carriage-drive. Then he dressed quickly in his smartest suit, filled his pockets with cash from a drawer, and next, knotting the sheets from his bed together and tying one end round the central mullion of the Tudor window which formed such a feature of his bedroom, he scrambled out, slid to the ground, and, taking the opposite direction to the Rat, marched off whistling a merry tune.

It was a gloomy luncheon for Rat when the Badger and the Mole returned. The Badger's remarks may be imagined; even the Mole could not help saying, "You've been a bit of a duffer this time, Ratty! Toad, too, of all animals!"

"He did it awfully well," said the crestfallen Rat.

"He did *you* awfully well!" rejoined the Badger hotly.

Meanwhile, Toad, gay and irresponsible, was walking along the high road, some miles from home. At first he had taken by-paths, and crossed many fields, and changed his course several times, in case of pursuit; but now, feeling safe from recapture, and the sun smiling brightly on him, and all nature joining in a chorus of approval to the song of self-praise his own heart was singing, he almost danced along the road in his satisfaction and conceit.

"Smart piece of work that!" he remarked to himself, chuckling. "Poor old Ratty! My! won't he catch it when the Badger gets back! A worthy fellow, Ratty, but very little intelligence and no education. I must take him in hand someday, and see if I can make something of him."

Full of conceited thoughts such as these, he strode along, his head in the air, till he reached a little town …

where the sign of "The Red Lion", swinging across the main street,

reminded him that he had not breakfasted that day.

He marched into the inn, ordered the best luncheon that could be provided, and sat down to eat it in the coffee-room.

He was about half-way through his meal when an only too familiar sound, approaching down the street, made him start trembling all over. The poop-poop! drew nearer, and the car could be heard to turn into the inn-yard and stop. Presently the party entered the coffee-room, talkative and gay, voluble on their experiences of the morning. Toad listened, all ears; at last he could stand it no longer. He slipped out of the room, paid his bill at the bar, and sauntered round to the inn-yard. "There cannot be any harm," he said to himself, "in my only just *looking* at it!"

The car stood in the middle of the yard, quite unattended. Toad walked slowly round it.

"I wonder," he said to himself presently, "I wonder if this sort of car *starts* easily?"

Next moment, hardly knowing how it came about, he found he had hold of the handle and was turning it. As the familiar sound broke forth, the old passion seized Toad and he found himself, somehow, seated in the driver's seat; as if in a dream, he pulled the lever and swung the car round the yard and out through the archway. He increased his pace, and as the car devoured the street and leapt forth on the high road through the open country, he was Toad once more, Toad at his best, Toad the terror, the traffic-queller, the Lord of the lone trail, before whom all must give way.

The miles were eaten up as he sped he knew not whither,

living his hour, reckless of what might come to him.

"To my mind," observed the Chairman of the Bench of Magistrates, "the *only* difficulty in this case is, how we can make it sufficiently hot for the rogue and hardened ruffian we see cowering in the dock before us.

"He has been found guilty of stealing a valuable motor-car; of driving to the public danger; and of gross impertinence to the rural police. Mr Clerk, tell us, please, what is the stiffest penalty we can impose for each of these offences?"

The Clerk scratched his nose with his pen. "Twelve months for the theft, three years for the furious driving and fifteen years for the cheek — those figures tot up to nineteen years — so you had better make it a round twenty and be on the safe side," he concluded.

"Excellent!" said the Chairman. "Prisoner! It's going to be twenty years for you this time. And mind, if you appear before us again, upon any charge whatever, we shall have to deal with you very seriously!"

The Toad was dragged from the Court House to the grim old castle, whose ancient towers soared high overhead. There in the heart of the innermost keep, the rusty key creaked in the lock, the great door clanged behind him; and Toad was a helpless prisoner in the remotest, best-guarded dungeon in all the length and breadth of Merry England.

SEVEN

Toad's Adventures

When Toad found himself in a dungeon, and knew that all the grim darkness of a medieval fortress lay between him and the world of sunshine and high roads where he had lately been so happy, he flung himself at full length on the floor, and shed bitter tears. "This is the end of everything," he said, "at least it is the end of Toad, which is the same thing. O unhappy and forsaken Toad!" He passed his days and nights for several weeks, refusing his meals or intermediate light refreshments, though the gaoler, knowing Toad's pockets were well lined, frequently pointed out that many comforts, indeed luxuries, could be sent in – at a price – from the outside.

Now the gaoler had a daughter. This kind-hearted girl said to her father one day, "I can't bear to see that poor beast so unhappy and getting so thin! You let me have the managing of him. I'll make him eat."

Her father replied that she could do what she liked with him. He was tired of Toad and his sulks. So she went and knocked on the door of Toad's cell.

"Cheer up, Toad," she said, entering. "Sit up and try a bit of dinner. See, I've brought you some of mine, hot from the oven!"

It was bubble-and-squeak, between two plates, and its fragrance filled the narrow cell. The penetrating smell of cabbage reached the nose of Toad as he lay prostrate in his misery on the floor, and gave him the idea for a moment that life was not such a desperate thing as he had imagined. But still he wailed, and kicked his legs, and refused to be comforted. So the wise girl retired, but, of course, the smell of hot cabbage remained, as it will do, and Toad, between sobs, sniffed and reflected and gradually began to think new thoughts; of chivalry and poetry, and deeds still to be done; of meadows, and cattle browsing in them; kitchen-gardens, and straight herb-borders, and warm snap-dragon beset by bees. The air of the cell took on a rosy tinge: he began to think of his friends, and how they would surely be able to do something; of lawyers, and what an ass he had been not to get a few; and lastly, he thought of his own cleverness and resource, and all that he was capable of if he only gave his great mind to it; and the cure was almost complete.

When the girl returned, some hours later, she carried a tray, with a cup of tea steaming on it; and a plate piled up with hot buttered toast. The smell of that toast simply talked to Toad; talked of warm kitchens; breakfast on bright frosty mornings, cosy firesides on winter evenings, when one's ramble was over and slippered feet were propped on the fender. Toad sat up, dried his eyes, sipped his tea and munched his toast, and soon began talking freely about himself, and the house he lived in, his doings there, and what a lot his friends thought of him.

The gaoler's daughter encouraged him to go on.

"Tell me about Toad Hall," she said. "It sounds beautiful. But first wait till I fetch you some more tea and toast."

She tripped away, and returned with a fresh trayful; and Toad, pitching in, told her about the boathouse, the fish-pond and the old walled kitchen-garden; about the pig-sties and the stables, the pigeon-house, and the hen-house; and about the dairy and the wash-house, the china cupboards, and the linen-presses (she liked that bit especially); about the banqueting hall, and the fun they had there when the other animals were gathered round the table and Toad was at his best, singing songs, telling stories, carrying on generally. Then she wanted to know about his friends, and was very interested in all he had to tell her about them and how they were, and what they did to pass their time. When she said good night, having filled his water-jug and shaken up his straw for him, Toad curled himself up and had an excellent night's rest and the pleasantest of dreams.

They had many interesting talks together as the dreary days went on; and the gaoler's daughter grew very sorry for Toad, and thought it a shame that a poor animal should be locked up in prison for what seemed to her a trivial offence.

One morning she said, "Toad, listen. I have an aunt who is a washerwoman."

"Never mind," said Toad affably. "*I* have several aunts who *ought* to be washerwomen."

"Do be quiet, Toad," said the girl. "As I said, I have an aunt; she does the washing for the prisoners in this castle. Now, she's very poor. A few pounds would mean a lot to her. If you could come to some arrangement by which she would let you have her dress and bonnet, you could escape from the castle as the official washerwoman. You're very alike in many respects –

particularly about the figure."

"We're *not*," said Toad. "I have a very elegant figure – for what I am."

"So has my aunt," replied the girl, "for what *she* is. But have it your own way. You horrid, proud, ungrateful animal, when I'm sorry for you, and trying to help you!"

"Yes, yes, thank you very much indeed," said Toad. "But look here! you wouldn't surely have Toad, of Toad Hall, going about the country disguised as a washerwoman!"

"Then you can stop here as Toad," replied the girl.

Toad was always ready to admit himself in the wrong. "You are a good, kind, clever girl," he said, "and I am a stupid toad. Introduce me to your worthy aunt, if you will be so kind."

Next evening the girl ushered her aunt into Toad's cell, bearing his week's washing pinned up in a towel. The sight of certain gold sovereigns thoughtfully placed on the table left little to discuss. In return for his cash, Toad received a cotton print gown, an apron, a shawl and a rusty black bonnet; the only stipulation the old lady made being that she should be gagged and bound and dumped in a corner.

"Now, Toad," said the girl. "Take off that coat and waist-coat of yours; you're fat enough as it is."

Shaking with laughter, she proceeded to "hook-and-eye" him into the gown, arranged the shawl with a professional fold, and tied the bonnet
under his chin.

"You're the very image of her," she giggled, "only I'm sure you never looked so respectable in all your life. Now, good-bye, Toad, and good luck. Go straight down the way you came up; and if anyone says anything to you, as they probably will, being men, you can chaff back a bit, of course, but remember you're a widow woman, with a character to lose."

With a quaking heart, Toad set forth on what seemed to be a hare-brained and hazardous undertaking; but he was soon surprised to find how easy everything was made for him. The washerwoman's squat figure in its familiar cotton print seemed a passport for every barred door and grim gateway; even when he hesitated, uncertain as to the right turning to take, he found himself helped by the warder at the next gate, anxious to be off to his tea, summoning him to come along sharp and not keep him waiting all night.

At last he heard
the wicket-gate in the
great outer door click behind
him, felt the air of the outer world
upon his brow, and knew that he was free!

Dizzy with the easy success of his daring exploit, he walked quickly towards the town. As he walked along, his attention was caught by some red and green lights a little way off, and the sound of puffing and snorting of engines fell on his ear. "Aha!" he thought, "this is a piece of luck! A railway-station."

He made his way to the station, consulted a time-table, and found that a train, bound more or less in the direction of home, was due to start in half an hour. "More luck!" said Toad, and went off to the booking-office to buy his ticket.

He gave the name of the station nearest Toad Hall, and put his fingers where his waistcoat pocket should have been and found – not only no money, but no pocket to hold it, and no waistcoat to hold the pocket!

To his horror he recollected that he had left both coat and waistcoat behind him in his cell, and with them his money, keys, matches, watch, pencil-case – all that makes life worth living. He made one desperate effort to carry the thing off, and, in his fine old manner he said, "Look here! I find I've left my purse behind. Just give me that ticket, will you, and I'll send the money on tomorrow. I'm well known in these parts."

The clerk stared at him and the rusty black bonnet. "I should think you were well known," he said, "if you've tried this game often. Stand away from the window, madam; you're obstructing the other passengers!"

Baffled and full of despair, he wandered down the platform where the train was standing and tears trickled down his nose.

"Hullo, mother!" said the engine-driver, "what's the trouble?

You don't look particularly cheerful!"

"O, sir!" said Toad, "I am a poor unhappy washerwoman, and I've lost all my money, and can't pay for a ticket, and I *must* get home tonight somehow, and whatever I am to do I don't know. O dear, O dear!"

"That's a bad business," said the engine-driver. "Lost your money – and can't get home – and got some kids, too, waiting for you, I dare say?"

"Any amount," sobbed Toad. "And they'll be hungry – and playing with matches – and upsetting lamps – and quarrelling. O dear, O dear!"

"I'll tell you what," said the good engine-driver. "You're a washerwoman. And I'm an engine-driver and there's no denying it's terribly dirty work. If you'll wash a few shirts for me when you get home, and send 'em along, I'll give you a ride on my engine. It's against the Company's regulations, but we're not so particular in these out-of-the-way parts."

Toad scrambled up into the cab of the engine. Of course, he had never washed a shirt in his life, and couldn't if he tried; but he thought: "When I get home to Toad Hall, and have money again, and pockets to put it in, I will send the engine-driver enough to pay for quite a quantity of washing, and that will be the same thing, or better."

The guard waved his welcome flag, the engine-driver whistled in cheerful response, and the train moved out of the station. As the speed increased, and Toad could see fields, and hedges, and cows, and horses, all flying past him, and as he thought how every minute was bringing him nearer to Toad Hall and friends, and money to chink in his pocket, and a soft bed to sleep in, and good things to eat, and praise and admiration of his adventures and his cleverness, he began to skip up and down and sing snatches of song, to the great astonishment of the engine-driver, who had come across washerwomen before, but never one like this.

They had covered many a mile, and Toad was considering what he would have for supper, when he noticed the engine-driver, with a puzzled expression on his face, was leaning over the side of the engine, listening hard. "It's strange," he said, "we're the last train running tonight, yet I could be sworn I heard another following us."

A dull pain in the lower part of Toad's spine made him want to sit down and try not to think of all the possibilities.

By this time the moon was shining brightly, and presently the engine-driver called out, "I can see it now! It's an engine. It looks as if we're being pursued."

The miserable Toad, crouching in the coal-dust, tried hard to think of something to do, with dismal want of success.

"They are gaining on us fast!" cried the engine-driver. "And the engine is crowded with the queerest lot of people! Warders and policemen all waving and shouting the same thing —

"Stop, stop, stop!"

Toad fell on his knees and cried, "Save me, save me, Mr Engine-driver, I am not the washerwoman I seem to be! I am a toad; and I have just escaped from a loathsome dungeon; and if those fellows on that engine recapture me, it will be chains and bread-and-water misery once more."

The engine-driver looked down on him very sternly, and said, "Now tell the truth; what were you put in prison for?"

"It was nothing much," said Toad, colouring deeply. "I only borrowed a motor-car. I didn't mean to steal it, really."

The engine-driver looked very grave and said, "By rights I ought to give you up. But I don't hold with motor-cars, and I don't hold with being ordered about on my own engine. So cheer up, Toad! I'll do my best, and we may beat them yet!"

They piled on more coals, shovelling furiously; the furnace roared, the sparks flew, the engine leapt and swung, but still their pursuers gained. The engine-driver wiped his brow and said, "It's no good, Toad. They are running light and have the better engine. There's just one thing left to do, it's your only chance, so be ready to jump when I tell you."

The train shot into a tunnel, and the engine roared and rattled, till they shot out at the other end. The driver shut off steam and braked, and as the train slowed down he called, "Now, jump!"

Toad jumped, rolled down a short embankment, picked himself up unhurt, scrambled into a wood and hid.

Peeping out, he saw his train get up speed and disappear at a great pace. Then out of the tunnel burst the pursuing engine, roaring and whistling, her motley crew waving and shouting, "Stop! stop! stop!" When they were past, Toad had a hearty laugh – for the first time since he was thrown into prison.

But he soon stopped when he came to consider that it was now very late and dark and cold, and he was in an unknown wood, with no money and no supper, and still far from friends and home; and the dead silence of everything, after the roar and rattle of the train, was something of a shock.

An owl, swooping towards him, brushed his shoulder with its wing, making him jump. Once he met a fox, who stopped, looked him up and down in a sarcastic sort of way, and said, "Hullo, washerwoman! Half a pair of socks and a pillow-case short this week! Mind it doesn't occur again!" and swaggered off, sniggering. At last he sought the shelter of a hollow tree, where he made himself as comfortable a bed as he could and slept soundly till morning.

— EIGHT —

The Further Adventures of Toad

The door of the hollow tree faced eastwards, so Toad was called at an early hour. Sitting up, he rubbed his eyes, looking round for familiar stone wall and barred window; then, with a leap of the heart, remembered everything – his escape, his flight, his pursuit; best of all, that he was free!

Free! He marched forth into the morning sun. He had the world to himself, that early summer morning. The dewy woodland was solitary and still; the green fields were his own to do as he liked with; the road, when he reached it, in that loneliness that was everywhere, seemed to be looking for company. Toad, however, was looking for something that could tell him clearly which way he ought to go.

The road was presently joined by a little canal. Round a bend in the canal came plodding a solitary horse, stooping forward as if in anxious thought. From his collar stretched a long line, taut, but dipping with his stride, the further part of it dripping pearly drops. Toad let the horse pass, and stood waiting for what the fates were sending him.

With a swirl of water, the barge slid up alongside of him, its occupant a big stout woman wearing a linen sun-bonnet.

"A nice morning, ma'am!" she remarked to Toad.

"I dare say it *is*, ma'am!" responded Toad, "to them that's not in trouble, like what I am. My married daughter, she sends for me to come at once; so off I comes, fearing the worst, as you will understand, ma'am, if you're a mother too. And I've left my washing business to look after itself, and my young children, ma'am; and I've lost all my money, and my way."

"Where might your married daughter be living, ma'am?" asked the barge-woman.

"Near Toad Hall, ma'am," replied Toad.

"Toad Hall? I'm going that way," replied the barge-woman. "Come along in the barge with me, and I'll give you a lift."

She steered the barge close to the bank, and Toad stepped lightly on board.

"So you're in the washing business?" said the barge-woman. "And are you *very* fond of washing?"

"I love it," said Toad. "I simply dote on it. Never so happy as when I've got both arms in the wash-tub."

"What a bit of luck," observed the barge-woman.

"Why, what do you mean?" asked Toad nervously.

"Well, there's a heap of things of mine that you'll find in a corner of the cabin. If you'll just put them through the wash-tub as we go along, it'll be a real help to me."

"I might not do 'em as you like," said Toad. "I'm more used to gentlemen's things myself. It's my special line."

"You do the washing you are so fond of," replied the barge-woman. "Don't deprive me of the pleasure of giving you a treat!"

Toad was fairly cornered. He looked for escape, saw he was too far from the bank for a flying leap, and resigned himself to his fate. "If it comes to that," he thought in desperation, "I suppose any fool can *wash*!"

He fetched tub, soap, and other necessaries from the cabin, selected a few garments, and set to.

A half-hour passed, and every minute of it saw Toad getting crosser and crosser. Nothing he could do to the things seemed to do them good. He tried coaxing, slapping, punching. His back ached and he noticed with dismay that his paws were beginning to get all crinkly. Now Toad was very proud of his paws. He muttered under his breath words that should never pass the lips of washerwomen or Toads; and lost the soap, for the fiftieth time.

The barge-woman laughed till tears ran down her cheeks.

"Pretty washerwoman you are!" she gasped. "Never washed so much as a dish-clout in your life, I'll lay!"

Toad's temper, which had been simmering for some time, now boiled over.

"You common, low, *fat* barge-woman!" he shouted; "don't you dare to talk to your betters like that! Washerwoman indeed! I would have you know that I am a Toad, a very well-known, respected, distinguished Toad! I may be under a bit of a cloud at present, but I will *not* be laughed at by a barge-woman!"

The woman peered under his bonnet. "Why, so you are!" she cried. "Well, I never! a horrid, nasty, crawly Toad! And in my nice clean barge, too! That is a thing that I will *not* have."

One big mottled arm shot out and caught Toad by a fore-leg. Then the world turned upside down, the barge seemed to flit across the sky, and Toad found himself flying through the air.

The water, when he reached it, proved cold, though not enough to quell his spirit. He rose to the surface, and when he had wiped the duckweed out of his eyes the first thing he saw was the barge-woman looking back at him over the stern of the barge and laughing.

He struck out for the shore, touched land, and climbed up the steep bank. Then, gathering his wet skirts well over his arms, he started to run after the barge, as fast as his legs would carry him, wild for revenge.

The barge-woman was still laughing when he drew up level with her. "Put yourself through your mangle, washerwoman," she called out, "and iron your face and crimp it, and you'll pass for quite a decent-looking Toad!"

Toad never paused to reply. Revenge was what he wanted, not cheap, windy, verbal triumphs, though he had a thing or two he would have liked to say. Running swiftly on he overtook the horse, unfastened the tow-rope, jumped on the horse's back, and urged it to a gallop by kicking it vigorously in the sides. He steered for the open country, abandoning the tow-path, and swinging his steed down a rutty lane. "Stop, stop, stop!" shouted the barge-woman.

"I've heard that song before," said Toad, laughing,

as he continued to spur his steed onward.

The barge-horse was not capable of any sustained effort, and its gallop soon subsided into a trot, and its trot to an easy walk; but Toad was quite contented with this. He had recovered his temper, now he had done something he thought really clever; and he was satisfied to jog along quietly in the sun, trying to forget how very long it was since he had had a square meal.

He had travelled some miles, his horse and he, and he was feeling drowsy in the hot sunshine, when the horse stopped, lowered his head, and began to nibble the grass; and Toad just saved himself from falling off.

He looked about him and found he was on a wide common,
dotted with patches of gorse and bramble as far as he could see.
Near him stood a dingy gipsy caravan, and a man was sitting,
very busy smoking and staring into the wide world.
A fire of sticks was burning near by, and over the fire
hung an iron pot, and out of that pot came forth
smells – warm, rich, and varied smells.
Toad sniffed, and looked at
the gipsy; and the
gipsy smoked,
and looked
at him.

Presently the gipsy took his pipe out of his mouth and remarked in a careless way, "Want to sell that there horse of yours?"

It had not occurred to Toad to turn the horse into cash.

"What?" he said, "me sell this beautiful young horse of mine? O no," he said, "it's out of the question. I'm too fond of him, and he dotes on me. All the same, how much might you be disposed to offer me?"

The gipsy looked the horse over, and he looked Toad over with equal care. "Shillin' a leg," he said briefly.

"A shilling a leg?" cried Toad. "I must work that out."

He climbed down off his horse and did sums on his fingers. At last he said, "That comes to four shillings. O no; I could not think of accepting four shillings for this young horse of mine."

"Well," said the gipsy, "I'll make it five shillings, and that's three-and-sixpence more than the animal's worth."

Toad pondered. He was hungry and penniless, and still some way from home, and enemies might be looking for him. To one in such a situation, five shillings may very well appear a large sum of money. On the other hand, it did not seem very much to get for a horse. But then, the horse hadn't cost him anything. At last he said firmly, "You hand me six shillings and sixpence, and as much breakfast as I can eat out of that iron pot of yours. In return, I will make over to you my spirited young horse, with all the harness and trappings on him, freely thrown in. If that's not good enough, say so, and I'll be getting on. I know a man near here who's wanted this horse for years."

The gipsy grumbled frightfully, and declared he'd be ruined. But in the end he lugged a dirty canvas bag out of the depths of his trouser-pocket, and counted out six shillings and sixpence into Toad's paw. Then he disappeared into the caravan, and returned with a large iron plate. He tilted the pot, and a stream of hot rich stew gurgled into it. Toad took the plate on his lap, and stuffed, and stuffed, and stuffed, and kept asking for more, and the gipsy never grudged it him. He thought he had never eaten so good a breakfast in all his life.

When Toad had taken as much stew on board as he thought he could possibly hold, he got up and said goodbye to the gipsy, and took an affectionate farewell of the horse; and the gipsy, who knew the riverside well, gave him directions which way to go, and he set forth on his travels again in the best possible spirits. He was, indeed, a very different Toad from the animal of an hour ago. The sun was shining brightly, his wet clothes were quite dry, he had money in his pockets once more, he was nearing home and friends and safety, and he had had a substantial meal, hot and nourishing, and felt big, and strong, and self-confident.

As he tramped along gaily, he thought of his adventures and escapes, and how when things seemed at their worst he had always managed to find a way out; and his pride and conceit began to swell within him. "Ho, ho!" he said to himself as he marched along with his chin in the air, "what a clever Toad I am! There is surely no animal equal to me for cleverness in the whole world! My enemies shut me up in prison, encircled by sentries, watched night and day by warders; I walk out through them all, by sheer ability coupled with courage. They pursue me with engines, and policemen, and revolvers; I snap my fingers at them, and vanish, laughing, into space. I am unfortunately thrown into a canal by an evil-minded woman. What of it? I swim ashore, I seize her horse, I ride off in triumph, and I sell the horse for a whole pocketful of money and an excellent breakfast! Ho, ho! I am The Toad, the handsome, the popular, the successful Toad!" He got so puffed up with conceit that he made up a song as he walked in praise of himself, and sang it at the top of his voice, though there was no one to hear it but him. It was perhaps the most conceited song that any animal ever composed:

The world has held great Heroes,
  As history-books have showed;
But never a name to go down to fame
  Compared with that of Toad!

The clever men at Oxford
  Know all that there is to be knowed.
But they none of them know one half as much
  As intelligent Mr Toad!

The animals sat in the Ark and cried,
  Their tears in torrents flowed.
Who was it said, "There's land ahead"?
  Encouraging Mr Toad!

The Army all saluted
  As they marched along the road.
Was it the King? Or Kitchener?
  No. It was Mr Toad.

The Queen and her Ladies-in-waiting
  Sat at the window and sewed.
She cried, "Look! who's that handsome *man?"*
  They answered, "Mr Toad."

There was a great deal more, but too dreadfully conceited to be written down. These are some of the milder verses.

He sang as he walked, and walked as he sang. But his pride was shortly to have a severe fall.

After some miles he reached the high road, and as he turned into it and glanced along its white length, he saw approaching him a speck that turned into a dot and then a blob, and then into something very familiar; and a "poop, poop!" fell on his delighted ear.

"This is something like!" said the excited Toad. "This is real life again, this is the world from which I have been missed so long! I will hail them, my brothers of the wheel, and they will give me a lift, and, with luck, it may even end in my driving up to Toad Hall! That will be one in the eye for Badger!"

He stepped out into the road to hail the motor-car, which came along at an easy pace, when suddenly he became very pale, his knees shook, and he doubled up with a sickening pain in his interior. And well he might, for the approaching car was the very one he had stolen out of the yard of the Red Lion Hotel! And the people in it were the very same people he had sat and watched at luncheon in the coffee-room!

He sank down in a heap, murmuring, "It's all up! Prison again! Dry bread and water!"

The motor-car drew nearer till at last he heard it stop. Two gentlemen got out and one of them said, "O dear! this is very sad! A poor washerwoman has fainted in the road! Perhaps she is overcome by the heat, poor creature. Let us lift her into the car and take her to the nearest village, where doubtless she has friends."

They tenderly lifted Toad into the motor-car and propped him up with soft cushions, and proceeded on their way.

When Toad knew that he was not recognized, his courage began to revive, and he opened first one eye, then the other.

"Look!" said one of the gentlemen, "she is better already. The fresh air is doing her good. How do you feel now, ma'am?"

"Thank you kindly, sir," said Toad in a feeble voice, "I'm feeling a great deal better! I was thinking, if I might sit on the front seat there, beside the driver, where I could get the fresh air full in my face, I should soon be all right again."

"What a sensible woman!" said the gentleman. "Of course you shall." So they helped Toad into the front seat beside the driver, and on they went once more.

Toad was almost himself again by now. And he turned to the driver at his side. "Please, sir," he said, "I wish you would let me try and drive a little, it looks so easy and I should like to be able to tell my friends that once I had driven a motor-car!"

The driver laughed so heartily that the gentleman inquired what the matter was. When he heard he said, "Bravo, ma'am! I like your spirit. Let her have a try."

Toad scrambled into the driver's seat, took the steering-wheel in his hands, listened to the instructions given him, and set the car in motion, very slowly and carefully.

The gentlemen behind clapped their hands and applauded, saying, "How well she does it! Fancy a washerwoman driving a car as well as that, the first time!"

Toad went a little faster; then faster still, and faster.

He heard the gentlemen call out, "Be careful, washerwoman!" And this annoyed him, and he began to lose his head.

The driver tried to interfere, but he pinned him down with one elbow, and put on full speed. "Washerwoman, indeed!" he shouted recklessly. "Ho, ho! I am the Toad, the motor-car snatcher, the prison-breaker, the Toad who always escapes!" With a cry of horror the party flung themselves on him. "Seize him!" they cried. "Seize the Toad who stole our motor-car!"

Alas! they should have remembered to stop the motor-car before playing pranks of that sort. With a half-turn of the wheel Toad sent the car crashing through the low roadside hedge. One mighty bound, a violent shock, and the wheels of the car were churning up the thick mud of a horse-pond.

Toad found himself flying through the air with the delicate curve of a swallow. He liked the motion, and was just beginning to wonder whether he would develop wings when he landed with a thump, in the soft rich grass of a meadow. Sitting up, he could just see the car in the pond; the gentlemen and driver were floundering helplessly in the water. He picked himself up and set off running across country as hard as he could, till he was breathless and weary, and had to settle into an easy walk. When he had recovered his breath and was able to think calmly, he began to laugh, and he laughed till he had to sit down under a hedge. "Ho, ho!" he cried. "Toad, as usual comes out on top! Who got them to give him a lift? Who persuaded them into letting him drive? Who landed them all in a horse-pond? Who escaped, flying gaily through the air, leaving them in the mud? Why, Toad, of course; clever Toad, great Toad, *good* Toad! How clever I am! How clever, how very clev—"

A slight noise behind him made him turn his head and look. O horror!

About two fields off, a chauffeur in his leather gaiters and two large rural policemen were running towards him as hard as they could go!

Toad pelted away again. "O my!" he gasped. "O my! O my!"

He glanced back, and saw to his dismay that they were gaining on him. On he ran. He did his best, but he was a fat animal, and his legs were short, and still they gained. He could hear them close behind him now. He struggled on wildly, looking back over his shoulder at the enemy, when suddenly the earth failed under his feet, he grasped at the air, and —

splash! he found himself head over ears in deep, rapid water;

in his panic he had run straight into the river!

He rose to the surface and tried to grasp the reeds and rushes that grew along the water's edge, but the stream was so strong it tore them out of his hands. "O my!" gasped Toad, "if ever I steal a motor-car again!" – then down he went, and came up breathless and spluttering. Presently he saw a big dark hole in the bank, just above his head, and as the stream bore him past, he reached up and caught hold of the edge and held on. Slowly and with difficulty he drew himself up out of the water. There he remained for some minutes, puffing and panting.

As he stared before him into the dark hole, some bright small thing shone and twinkled in its depths, moving towards him.

A face grew up around it, a familiar face!

Brown and small, with whiskers.

Grave and round, with neat ears and silky hair.

It was the Water Rat!

NINE

The Return of Toad

The Rat put out a paw, gripped Toad by the scruff of the neck, and gave a great hoist and pull; and the waterlogged Toad came up over the edge of the hole till at last he stood in the hall, streaked with mud and weed, but happy and high-spirited, now that he found himself once more in the house of a friend.

"O Ratty!" he cried. "I've been through such times since I saw you last, you can't think! Just hold on till I tell you—"

"Toad," said the Water Rat, "go upstairs at once, and take off that old cotton rag that looks as if it belonged to some washer-woman. I'll have something to say to you later!"

Toad was at first inclined to stop and do some talking back at him. He had had enough of being ordered about in prison. However, he caught sight of himself in the looking-glass over the hatstand, with the rusty black bonnet perched rakishly over one eye, and he changed his mind and went very quickly upstairs to the Rat's dressing-room.

By the time he came down again luncheon was on the table. While they ate, Toad told the Rat all his adventures. The more he talked, the more grave and silent the Rat became.

When at last Toad had talked himself to a standstill, the Rat said, "Now, Toady, seriously, don't you see what an ass you've been making of yourself? You've been handcuffed, imprisoned, starved, chased, insulted and ignominiously flung into the water. Where's the amusement in that? Where does the fun come in? And all because you must needs go and steal a motor-car. You've never had anything but trouble from the moment you set eyes on one. Think of your friends. Do you suppose it's any pleasure to me to hear animals saying I'm the chap that keeps company with gaol-birds?"

Toad heaved a deep sigh and said, "Quite right, Ratty! I've been a conceited ass, I can see that. As for motor-cars, I've not been so keen about them since my last ducking in that river of yours. The fact is, I've had enough of adventures. I shall lead a quiet life, pottering about Toad Hall; and I shall keep a pony-chaise to jog about the country in, as I used to in the old days."

"Do you mean you haven't *heard*?" cried the Rat.

"Heard what?" said Toad, turning pale.

"About the Stoats and Weasels?"

"No!" cried Toad. "What have they been doing?"

"They've been and taken Toad Hall!"

A large tear welled up in each of Toad's eyes, overflowed and splashed on the table, plop! plop!

"When you got into that − trouble of yours," said the Rat, "it was a good deal talked about down here. Animals took sides. The River-bankers stuck up for you. But the Wild Wood animals said hard things, served you right. You were done for this time! You would never come back again, never! And one night, a band of weasels and ferrets and stoats broke into Toad Hall, and have been living there ever since!"

"O, have they!" said Toad, getting up and seizing a stick. "I'll jolly soon see about that!"

"It's no good!" called the Rat after him. "You'll only get into trouble."

But there was no holding the Toad. He marched down the road, his stick over his shoulder, till he got near his front gate, when suddenly there popped up from behind the palings a long yellow ferret with a gun.

"Who comes there?" said the ferret sharply.

"What do you mean by talking like that to me?" said Toad very angrily. "Come out or I'll—"

The ferret said never a word, but brought his gun to his shoulder. Toad dropped flat in the road and *Bang!* a bullet whistled over his head. The startled Toad scrambled to his feet and scampered down the road; and as he ran he heard the ferret laughing a horrid, thin little laugh.

He went back, got out the boat, and set off rowing up river to where the garden of Toad Hall came down to the waterside.

Arriving within sight of his old home, he rested on his oars

and surveyed the land cautiously.

All seemed very peaceful and deserted. He would try the boat-house first, he thought. Very warily he paddled up the creek, and was just passing under the bridge, when ... *Crash!*

A great stone, dropped from above, smashed through the bottom of the boat. It filled and sank, and Toad found himself struggling in deep water. Looking up, he saw two stoats leaning over the parapet of the bridge, watching him with glee. "It will be your head next time, Toady!" they called out to him. Toad swam to shore while the stoats laughed and laughed.

"Well, *what* did I tell you?" said the Rat crossly, when Toad related his disappointing experiences. "And now you've been and lost me my boat! And simply ruined that nice suit I lent you! Really, Toad, be patient. We can do nothing until we have seen the Mole and the Badger."

"O, ah, yes, the Mole and the Badger," said Toad. "What's become of the dear fellows? I had forgotten all about them."

"Well may you ask!" said the Rat reproachfully. "While you were riding about in motor-cars, and breakfasting on the fat of the land, those two animals have been camping out in every sort of weather, watching over your house, contriving how to get it back for you. You don't deserve such loyal friends, Toad, you don't, really."

"I know," sobbed Toad. "Let me go and find them, and share their hardships, and— Hold on! Supper's here, hooray!"

They had just finished their meal when there came a heavy knock at the door, and in walked Mr Badger. His shoes were covered with mud, and he was looking rough and tousled; but then he had never been very smart, Badger. He came solemnly up to Toad, shook him by the paw, and said, "Welcome home, Toad!" Then he helped himself to a large slice of cold pie.

Presently there came another, lighter knock and the Rat ushered in the Mole, very shabby and unwashed, with bits of hay and straw sticking in his fur.

"Toad!" cried the Mole, beaming. "Fancy having you back! We never dreamt you would turn up so soon! Why, you must have managed to escape, you clever Toad!"

The Rat pulled him by the elbow; but it was too late.

"Clever? O no!" said Toad. "Not according to my friends. I've only broken out of the strongest prison in England, that's all! And captured a railway train and escaped on it, that's all! And disguised myself and gone about the country humbugging everybody, that's all! O no! I'm a stupid ass, I am!"

He straddled the hearth-rug, thrust his paw into his pocket and pulled out a handful of silver. "Look at that!" he cried, displaying it. "Not bad for a few minutes' work! And how do you think I done it, Mole? Horse-dealing! That's how!"

"Toad, be quiet!" said the Rat. "And don't you egg him on, Mole, when you know what he is; tell us what the position is, now Toad is back at last."

"About as bad as it can be," replied the Mole. "Badger and I have been round and round the place; always the same thing. Sentries posted everywhere, guns poked out at us, always an animal on the look-out, and when they see us, my! how they laugh! That's what annoys me most!"

The Badger, having finished his pie, got up from his seat and stood before the fireplace.

"Toad!" he said severely. "You bad little animal! Aren't you ashamed of yourself? Think what your father would have said if he had been here tonight, and known of all your goings-on! What Mole says is true. The stoats are on guard, at every point. It's quite useless to think of attacking the place."

"Then it's all over," sobbed the Toad. "I shall go and enlist for a soldier, and never see my dear Toad Hall any more!"

"Cheer up, Toady!" said the Badger. "There are more ways of getting back a place than taking it by storm. I haven't said my last word yet. Now I'm going to tell you a secret."

Toad dried his eyes. Secrets had an immense attraction for him, because he never could keep one.

"There – is – an – underground – passage," said the Badger impressively, "that leads from the river bank quite near here, right up into the middle of Toad Hall."

"Nonsense! Badger," said Toad airily. "You've been listening to some of the yarns they spin in the public-houses about here. I know every inch of Toad Hall, inside and out. Nothing of the sort, I do assure you!"

"My young friend," said the Badger with severity, "your father, who was a worthy animal – a lot worthier than some I know – was a particular friend of mine, and told me a great deal he wouldn't have dreamt of telling you. He discovered that passage – of course it was made hundreds of years before he ever came to live there – and he repaired it and cleaned it out, because he thought it might come in useful some day, in case of trouble or danger, and he showed it to me. 'Don't let my son know about it,' he said. 'He's a good boy, but simply cannot hold his tongue. If he's ever in a real fix, and it would be of use to him, you may tell him about the secret passage; but not before.'"

The other animals looked to see how Toad would take it.

"Well," he said, "perhaps I am a bit of a talker. A popular fellow such as I am – my friends get round me – and somehow my tongue gets wagging. I have the gift of conversation. I've been told I ought to have a *salon*, whatever that may be. Go on, Badger. How's this passage of yours going to help us?"

"I've found out a thing or two lately," continued the Badger. "There's going to be a big banquet tomorrow night. It's somebody's birthday – the Chief Weasel's, I believe – and all the weasels will be gathered in the dining-hall, eating and drinking and carrying on, suspecting nothing. No guns, no swords, no sticks, no arms of any sort whatever!"

"But the sentinels will be posted as usual," remarked the Rat.

"Exactly," said the Badger; "that is my point. The weasels will trust entirely to their sentinels. That is where the passage comes in. That useful tunnel leads right up under the butler's pantry, next to the dining-hall!"

"Aha! that squeaky board in the butler's pantry!" said Toad. "Now I understand it!"

"We shall creep out into the pantry—" cried the Mole.

"—with our pistols, swords and sticks—" shouted the Rat.

"— and rush in upon them," said the Badger.

"— and whack 'em,"

"and whack 'em,"

"and whack 'em!" cried the Toad in ecstasy, running round and round the room.

"Very well, then," said the Badger, "our plan is settled and there's nothing more to argue about. So, as it's getting late, all of you go off to bed at once. We will make the necessary arrangements in the morning."

Toad slept late next morning, and by the time he got down, found the other animals had finished their breakfast some time before. The Mole had slipped off by himself, without telling anyone where he was going. The Badger sat in the armchair, reading the paper, and the Rat was running round the room busily, distributing weapons in four little heaps on the floor.

Presently the Mole came tumbling into the room, evidently pleased with himself. "I've been having such fun!" he began; "I've been getting a rise out of the stoats!"

"I hope you've been careful, Mole?" said the Rat.

"I hope so, too," said the Mole. "I got the idea when I found Toad's old washerwoman-dress hanging in the kitchen. I put it on, and off I went to Toad Hall, as bold as you please. 'Good morning, gentlemen!' says I. 'Want any washing done today?'

"They looked at me very proud and stiff and haughty, and said, 'Go away, washerwoman! We don't do washing on duty.' 'Or any other time?' says I. Ho, ho, ho! Some of the stoats turned quite pink, and the sergeant said, 'Run away, my good woman!' 'Run away?' says I; 'it won't be me running away, in a very short time from now!'"

"O, *Moly*, how could you?" said the Rat, dismayed.

The Badger laid down his paper.

"I could see them pricking up their ears and looking at each other," went on the Mole; "and the sergeant said to them, 'Never mind *her*; she doesn't know what she's talking about.'

"'O! don't I?' said I. 'Well, my daughter washes for Mr Badger, and that'll show you whether I know! A hundred bloodthirsty Badgers are going to attack Toad Hall this very night, by way of the paddock. Six boat-loads of rats will come up the river while a picked body of toads, known as the Die-hards, or the Death-or-Glory Toads, will storm the orchard and carry everything before them. There won't be much left of you to wash, by the time they've done with you.' Then I ran away and hid;

and presently I came creeping back along the ditch and took a peep at them through the hedge. They were all as nervous as could be, running all ways at once, and I heard them saying 'That's *just* like the weasels; they're to stop comfortably in the banqueting-hall, and have feasting and songs and all sorts of fun, while we must stay on guard in the cold and dark, and be cut to pieces by bloodthirsty Badgers!'"

"You silly ass, Mole!" cried Toad. "You've been and spoilt everything!"

"Mole," said the Badger. "You have managed excellently. I begin to have great hopes of you. Clever Mole!"

The Toad was wild with jealousy, especially as he couldn't make out for the life of him what the Mole had done that was so clever; fortunately for him, before he could show temper, the bell rang for luncheon.

It was a simple but sustaining meal – bacon and broad beans, and a macaroni pudding; and when they had done, the Badger settled himself into an arm-chair, and said, "I'm just going to take forty winks, while I can." And he was soon snoring. The anxious Rat resumed his preparations, running between his heaps. So the Mole drew his arm through Toad's, led him into the open air, shoved him into a wicker chair, and made him tell all his adventures from beginning to end. Toad rather let himself go. Indeed, much he related belonged more to the category of what-might-have-happened-had-I-only-thought-of-it-in-time-instead-of-ten-minutes-afterwards. Those are always the best and the raciest adventures; and why should they not be ours, as much as the things that really come off?

When it began to grow dark, the Rat summoned them back into the parlour, stood each of them alongside his little heap, and proceeded to dress them up for the coming expedition. First, there was a belt to go round each animal, then a sword to be stuck into each belt, and then a cutlass on the other side to balance it. Then a pair of pistols, a policeman's truncheon, several sets of handcuffs, some bandages and sticking-plaster, and a flask and a sandwich-case. The Badger laughed and said, "I'm going to do all I've got to do with this here stick." But the Rat only said, "*Please*, Badger! You know I shouldn't like you to say I had forgotten *anything*!"

When all was quite ready, the Badger took a lantern in one paw, grasped his great stick with the other, and said, "Now then, follow me!"

The Badger led the animals along by the river for a little way, and then into a hole in the bank. At last they were in the secret passage, and the expedition had begun! It was low and narrow, and Toad began to shiver from dread of what might be before him. The lantern was far ahead, and he could not help lagging behind in the darkness. He heard the Rat call out "*Come* on, Toad!" and a terror seized him of being left alone, and he "came on" with such a rush that he upset the Rat into the Mole and the Mole into the Badger, and all was confusion. They groped and shuffled along, with their ears pricked up and their paws on their pistols, till at last the Badger said, "We ought to be nearly under the Hall."

Then suddenly they heard, far away as it might be, and yet nearly over their heads, shouting and cheering and stamping on the floor. Toad's terrors all returned, but the Badger only remarked, "They *are* going it, the weasels!"

The passage now began to slope upwards; and the noise broke out again, quite distinct this time, and very close above them. "Ooo-ray-oo-ray-oo-ray-ooray!" they heard, and the stamping of feet on the floor, and clinking of glasses as fists pounded on the table. "Come on!" said Badger. They hurried along till the passage came to a full stop, and they found themselves standing under the trap-door that led up into the butler's pantry.

The Badger said, "Now, boys, all together!" and they heaved the trap-door back.

The noise, as they emerged, was simply deafening. As the cheering and hammering slowly subsided, a voice could be made out saying, "Before I resume my seat I should like to say one word about our kind host, Mr Toad. We all know Toad! *Good* Toad, *modest* Toad, *honest* Toad!"

"Let me get at him!" muttered Toad, grinding his teeth.

"Hold hard a minute!" said the Badger, restraining him with difficulty. "Get ready, all of you!"

"Let me sing you a song," went on the voice, "which I have composed on the subject of Toad –" Then the Chief Weasel – for it was he – began in a high, squeaky voice:

> *Toad he went a-pleasuring*
> *Gaily down the street –*

The Badger drew himself up, took a firm grip of his stick, and cried: "Follow me!" And flung the door open.

My! What a squealing and squeaking filled the air!
Well might the weasels spring at the windows!
Well might the ferrets rush for the chimney!
Well might tables and chairs be upset,
and glass and china be sent crashing
on the floor, in the panic of that
terrible moment when the four
Heroes strode into the room!
The mighty Badger, his whiskers
bristling, his great cudgel whistling
through the air; Mole, black and grim,
brandishing his stick, shouting his
awful war-cry, "A Mole! A Mole!"
Rat, desperate and determined, his
belt bulging with weapons of every
age and variety; Toad, swollen to
twice his ordinary size, emitting
Toad-whoops that chilled them
to the marrow! "Toad he went
a-pleasuring!" he yelled.
"I'll pleasure 'em!" and
he went straight for
the Chief Weasel.

Up and down strode the four Friends, whacking every head that showed itself; and in five minutes the room was cleared. Through the broken windows the shrieks of escaping weasels were borne faintly to their ears; on the floor lay some dozen or so of the enemy, on whom the Mole was busily engaged in fitting handcuffs. The Badger wiped his brow.

"Mole," he said, "you're the best of fellows! Just cut along outside, and see what those sentries are doing. I've an idea, thanks to you, we shan't have much trouble from *them*!"

Then he said in that rather common way he had of speaking, "Stir your stumps, Toad! We've got your house back for you, and you don't offer us so much as a sandwich."

Toad felt hurt that the Badger didn't say pleasant things to him, as he had to the Mole, and tell him what a fine fellow he was, and how splendidly he had fought; for he was rather pleased with himself and the way he had sent the Chief Weasel flying across the table. But he bustled about, and so did the Rat, and soon they found some guava jelly in a glass dish, and a cold chicken, some trifle, and quite a lot of lobster salad; and in the pantry they came upon a basket of French rolls and any quantity of cheese, butter, and celery. They were just about to sit down when the Mole clambered in through the window, chuckling, with an armful of rifles.

"It's all over," he reported. "From what I can make out, as soon as the stoats, who were very nervous and jumpy already, heard the shrieks inside the hall, they threw down their rifles and fled. So *that's* all right!"

Then Toad, like the gentleman he was, put all jealousy from him and said, "Thank you, Mole, for your trouble tonight and especially for your cleverness this morning!" So they finished their supper in great joy and contentment, safe in Toad's ancestral home; won back by matchless valour, consummate strategy, and a proper handling of sticks.

After this climax, the four animals continued to lead their lives, undisturbed by further invasions.

Sometimes, in the long summer evenings, the friends would take a stroll together in the Wild Wood, now tamed so far as they were concerned; and it was pleasing to see how respectfully they were greeted by the inhabitants; mother-weasels would bring their young ones to the mouths of their holes, and say, pointing, "Look! There goes the great Mr Toad! And that's the Water Rat, a terrible fighter. And yonder comes the famous Mr Mole, of whom you've heard your father tell!" But when their infants were fractious and quite beyond control, they would quiet them by telling how, if they didn't hush, the terrible grey Badger would up and get them. This was a base libel on Badger, who, though he cared little about Society, was rather fond of children; but it never failed to have its full effect.

First published individually as *The Riverbank and Other Stories* (1996) and *The Adventures of Mr Toad* (1998) by Walker Books Ltd., 87 Vauxhall Walk, London, SE11 5HJ

First U.S. edition 2003

Library of Congress Cataloging-in-Publication Data
Moore, Inga.
The wind in the willows / written by Kenneth Grahame ;
abridged and illustrated by Inga Moore. — 1st U.S. ed.
p. cm.
Originally published: London ; Boston : Walker Books, 2000.
Summary: The escapades of four animal friends who live along a river in
the English countryside — Toad, Mole, Rat, and Badger.
ISBN 0-7636-2242-7
[1. Animals — Fiction.] I. Grahame, Kenneth, 1859–1932. II. Title.
PZ7.M7846Wi2003
[Fic] — dc21   2003044001

2 4 6 8 10 9 7 5 3 1

Printed in China

This book was typeset in M Bembo.
The illustrations were done in ink and pastel crayon.

Candlewick Press
2067 Massachusetts Avenue
Cambridge, Massachusetts 02140

visit us at www.candlewick.com